ALPHA KING

SARA FIELDS

Copyright © 2021 by Stormy Night Publications and Sara Fields

All rights reserved. No part of this book may be reproduced or transmitted in any form or by any means, electronic or mechanical, including photocopying, recording, or by any information storage and retrieval system, without permission in writing from the publisher.

Published by Stormy Night Publications and Design, LLC.
www.StormyNightPublications.com

Fields, Sara
Alpha King

Cover Design by Korey Mae Johnson
Images by Shutterstock/Augustino, Shutterstock/KeepWatch, Shutterstock/Rudy_agan, and Shutterstock/Holger Kirk

This book is intended for *adults only*. Spanking and other sexual activities represented in this book are fantasies only, intended for adults.

CHAPTER 1

awson

"Come on! We need to get out of the room. This thing is going to blow in like thirty seconds and I promise you don't want to be in the same room unless you want your ears ringing for the next year!" Genzo shouted. I hastily beckoned my men to follow me around the corner into the dark shroud of the tunnel and we got as far away from the detonation site as we could.

I took a deep breath, counting down the seconds until we breached the basement of the Venuti family fortress.

There was no doubt in my mind that this was going to work. I'd gotten my hands on the original blueprints for the fortified building, knowing that the only way in would be from beneath it. They'd buried their underground vault deep, but we'd dug deeper and found what would be one of the exterior walls of the massive skyscraper rooted below.

The Venuti had wronged my pack and I intended to fix that.

I would spare no expense to get my beta back. He'd been taken by the Venuti, and it was up to me to right their wrongs as the alpha of the Crescent Moon Pack. I had a reputation to uphold. I protected the members of my pack no matter what it took and that meant I had to rescue Toboe before the Venuti decided to kill him and start an all-out war between our two families.

Time seemed to slow, and I could almost sense the vibrations within the mechanism of the bomb about to engage. My heart pounded in my chest as I took a deep breath. I covered my ears.

Three.

Two.

One.

Boom!

A blast of dust, silt, and wet dirt exploded out of the doorway into the tunnel. We only waited a few seconds for most of it to settle before we charged into the room to see the damage. The walls the Venuti built were thick and it had taken quite of bit of explosive power to break through them. Mangled cement and steel practically smoked from the massive explosion, but there was a circular opening in the wall just large enough for us to make our way through one by one.

"Let's move. Those fuckers will have heard that," I growled, and my men smiled with exhilaration. They were looking forward to this, and to be honest so was I.

I stepped forward and dipped my head low enough so that I could make it through the opening without hitting the top. If

I wasn't so angry about my beta's kidnapping, I would have been impressed by the rather incredible feat of engineering that had gone into making an underground fortress like this beneath the silt and sand of New Orleans. I didn't much care about that now though. I just wanted to get him back.

I pressed forward and walked into a big room. The overhead lights were flickering, but that didn't stop me from pulling in a small gasp of shock at what was inside that vault.

There were so many gold bars. Stacks and stacks of them piled on heavy-duty metal shelving built right into the walls. I had known the Venuti clan of vampires had been around for centuries but seeing just a portion of their wealth right in front of my eyes like this was another thing altogether. They were known to have been a part of the Roman Empire, the British Empire, and so many others in between. They were opportunistic creatures, picking and choosing various human governments to infiltrate to build and maintain their power and wealth. In the past hundred years or so, they'd pulled back and maintained their position here in New Orleans. Clearly, they'd taken all that ancient wealth and compiled some of it here. I was certain that this just barely scratched the surface.

My men funneled in behind me single file as I heard each one of them react the same way I did.

"Damn. This is something else," Genzo whispered. "When we leave, I'm gonna snag one of these and buy my wife something nice."

I chuckled.

"Yeah, she probably deserves it for dealing with you all these years," I smirked, and he narrowed his eyes at me with mock anger.

"What do you mean, boss? I'm clearly a catch," he replied, and even though he tried to cover up his grin of amusement, ultimately he failed and started to laugh.

"You snore loud enough to wake the dead, Genzo," I said, my voice flat, and he broke out with a raucous laugh.

"No, I don't," he replied.

About a dozen men behind me voiced their disagreement with his words and I just grinned.

"Well. I'll just make it a hell of a good-sized diamond," he finally muttered with a chuckle.

"Good man," I said. With a quiet laugh, I stepped forward toward the door and slowly opened it, expecting to be ambushed. For a moment, I just listened. I heard nothing.

I'd expected the Venuti to move slowly. I'd specifically planned to make our entry point just after sunrise when most of the vampires were asleep. They would die if they went into the sun. They'd sizzle right up like overcooked bacon. Didn't smell particularly good.

I knew the vampires would come for us, but their reaction times would be slower right now in deploying a team to handle our infiltration. We had a small window to find and rescue Toboe from their clutches down here and we needed to take advantage of that.

"Follow me. The holding cells should be this way," I whispered. "From here on out, try to move as stealthily as you can. Let's make the most out of this."

My men nodded succinctly. They all understood how serious this was.

I crept into the hallway, keeping my footsteps light. Carefully, we made our way toward the prison. The door was locked, but Genzo was prepared for that. He reached into his bag and pulled out a rectangular box. He pressed it against the steel lock, and it stayed, held in place by powerful magnets, before he typed a short code into the watch on his wrist.

The box popped as a small explosion destroyed the lock and the door swung open. It was all very quiet and self-contained, perfectly designed for missions that required a more delicate touch. Genzo had quite a superior talent with explosives and most other technology, so much so that I sometimes wondered what I'd do without him.

I swung the door fully open and strode inside. This section of the fortress was two stories tall, lined with two rows of cells designed to hold vampires and shifters alike. The metal bars were thick and as I moved closer toward an empty cell, I reached out to touch them.

My skin sizzled hot and I sucked in a furious breath. I pulled my hand away and glared down at the angry burn on my fingertips. At once, my flesh began to pull back together, and within a few seconds there was nothing but unmarred skin left behind.

"The goddamn cells are silver," I growled.

"As expected, boss. I can handle that," Genzo whispered, and I nodded once in acknowledgement.

I wrinkled my nose, breathing in the rancid scent of the vampires imprisoned here. To my kind, they smelled of rotten fruit and putrid stinking meat. To them, we just smelled like wet dog.

Nearby, one of the prisoners snarled. Our presence had been noticed.

Knowing time was of the essence now, I walked down the line of cells. I was surprised by the number of vampires imprisoned down here, likely from other families or perhaps they were even Venuti if they'd broken ancient vampire law. Those cells weren't silver, but very thick ultra-hard steel strong enough to stand against the strength of their kind.

That wouldn't stop the likes of us. That's why they designed the ones meant for shifters with silver. It was our one weakness, and they took advantage of that as much as they could.

Having not found Toboe on the ground floor, I leapt up to the second. I vaulted over the iron railing and walked down the line until I finally saw the familiar blond hair of my beta. He was sitting on a cot in the back of the cell and when he saw me, he grinned.

"About time, Lawson," he chided quietly, and I chuckled.

"I should have just left you here," I smirked.

"Then who would you have to tell you that you look pretty every day?" he answered, and I snorted in response.

"Keep it up, Toboe. I've been thinking about promoting Genzo anyway," I answered, and Genzo chuckled by my side.

"Liar. I'm irreplaceable," Toboe grinned, and I just shook my head.

"What do you think, Genzo? Want to get out of here and find someplace to enjoy a nice steak?" I asked.

"Steak? Fuck, yeah. I always say yes to a good piece of beef," Genzo replied, and Toboe glared at me, but his eyes sparkled with his amusement. Toboe would always be my second in command, no matter how much shit he gave me. Being a beta was in his blood, just like being an alpha was in mine. No matter how useful Genzo was, he was an omega and that meant he was at the bottom of the pack hierarchy, and he would always answer to the two of us.

"The bars are silver," Toboe pointed out.

"No shit, Sherlock," Genzo grinned as he reached into his bag. "It's not like I was planning on pulling out the bars one by one with my goddamn hands."

Toboe shook his head. He hadn't stopped smirking.

Beside each cell was a digital panel that operated the door, opening and closing the cell with a code. Genzo would have to hack it to free Toboe. Firepower wasn't going to work here. He'd need a more subtle approach so that my beta didn't get hurt in the process.

"Get it done, Genzo," I finally ordered, and at once my men got down to business. Feeling a bit inquisitive, I walked down the line of vampire and shifter inmates, but I didn't recognize any of them. Some of them snarled at me, others looked on in curiosity, and yet others just trash-talked the Crescent Moon Pack as I walked by. I wasn't surprised by that. As the alpha of my pack, I was quite identifiable. I would have been more shocked if they hadn't known who I was.

At the end of the line, I came by an unexpected surprise.

A human female.

I stopped and peered into her cell. She stared back at me without a single ounce of fear.

That was... *unusual*.

"Keep walking, wolf. I'm not afraid of your kind," she challenged, and I stared more closely at her. Long ago, the vampire and shifter families had come together to create an ancient pact to keep our existence secret from mortals. There were humans in the world that knew of us, but they were few and far between.

She was young, perhaps in her mid-twenties. The fact that she could recognize me without seeing me shift was unexpected, to say the least.

I approached the cage, casually reaching for the bars. These ones weren't silver, and I could grasp them easily. They would be strong, sure, but no match for me. She wouldn't be safe in her cage from the likes of a beast like me.

I took several long moments to study her fiery gaze staring back at me. Her deep blue eyes nearly glittered with challenge. Her jawline was tense, but it did nothing to hide the beautiful curve of her high cheekbones and full pink lips. Her eyes were framed by exquisitely thick lashes. In the dim light, her dark mahogany hair still shone, lush and exquisitely long enough to reach at least the middle of her back, but with her sitting against the wall I couldn't be completely certain. She cocked her head as she watched me scrutinizing her and nearly snarled once my gaze dropped below her chin.

She was wearing a dark long-sleeve jacket and a dark shirt, but I could see enough to know that her breasts could fill each of my hands. Her hips curved in the most delicious way and her long legs were a sight to behold.

She was sinfully beautiful, and I breathed in deep, catching her scent for the first time.

My cock hardened almost immediately.

The aroma of fragrant wildflowers and brown sugar and vanilla swirled around me, holding me captive for several long moments before I managed to get ahold of myself. Carefully, I wrapped my fingers around an iron bar and cocked my head in her direction.

"What could the vampires want with a human like you?" I asked.

She shrugged, feigning indifference. I knew at once it was a lie. Everything in her body language screamed to me that she knew what she was here for. She just didn't want to tell me.

No matter.

"I can't imagine they'd let a pretty thing like you go. They'd drain you before they let you walk out their doors," I murmured. Her gaze hardened. I'd struck a nerve.

"They wouldn't dare kill me," she answered, and I raised an eyebrow in disbelief. Even though she knew we existed, that didn't change the fact that vampires and shifters were far more powerful than any human just by sheer strength alone. She wouldn't be able to fight off even a single one. She didn't have a chance.

Quickly, I glanced over at Genzo and my men. They were still hard at work on getting Toboe's cell open so that we could rescue him.

"Are you sure of that, human?" I asked carefully, turning my gaze back toward the furious eyes of the curious little package I'd happened to find locked away down here. If I left her, she'd be trapped in a viper's den of vampires. There was no way she'd ever get out of here alive.

The only chance she'd have was to come with my pack.

I grasped the bars of her cage and pulled on them hard, using my strength to bend them far enough apart so that she could slip through. She watched me with skepticism, studying my expression as I worked to free her. She didn't say a word, probably trying to figure out why a random shifter stranger would help free her from a vampire prison deep underground.

Once I bent the bars enough, which wasn't that much because she was pretty small, I took a step back and casually glanced at her.

"If you want to get out, you're welcome to come with us. If not, you're welcome to stay here and die with the Venuti," I offered.

I turned away and it was at that point that all hell broke loose.

Our presence had apparently been noticed.

The odor of vampire grew even stronger and more rank. There were at least two dozen coming for us, if not more.

I grinned. This was going to be a good fight.

I heard the tiny female scrambling behind me and I turned back. She shouldn't be here for this. I wouldn't allow it. I looked around and saw Lucas close by. I called out to him.

"Lucas, see to it she makes it out safely. I don't want her here when the fight breaks out. Take her and move," I ordered. Without a word, he obeyed me. He pushed past me and just when I turned my back, the sounds of a scuffle made me pause and look to see what possibly could be holding him up.

She was fighting him. He was a wolf shifter at least double her size and she was holding her own against him.

That was unheard of. I'd never seen or heard of anything like it.

Even though a small army of vampires were so close that the hair on the back of my neck was raised in alarm, I watched in awe as she spun out of his range and then back to just dip out of his grasp so that she could strike him.

She had a knife.

Where the fuck had she gotten a knife? Surely the vampires had searched her before they flung her in that cell. They'd have found any weapons on her.

Apparently, assuming that was wrong.

She fought him hard. There was a distinctly fluid motion to the way she fought, as if she could anticipate Lucas' movements before he made them. I watched her gaze studying him, so intently focused that I realized that was exactly what she was doing. She'd had training and a lot of it. I couldn't be certain exactly which martial arts she had studied, but her skill was impressive.

Honestly, it was a little arousing just to watch.

I couldn't help but smirk as I watched Lucas try to contend with the feisty little human. He'd clearly underestimated her, as had I, but I wasn't the one everyone would see fighting against her.

After this was over, the rest of the pack wouldn't ever let him live that down.

He tried to grab at her arm, and she slipped far enough away that she just barely escaped his reach. She didn't make a run for it as I would have expected. Instead, she moved in with her knife with brutal intent. She slashed at him, her movement extremely precise.

I crossed my arms, enjoying the show. If she managed to cut him, it wouldn't much matter. Getting slashed with a knife was certainly no walk in the park. It would hurt, but he'd heal almost instantly. Our healing abilities were insanely useful for things like that.

As I expected, he didn't jerk out of the way. He'd thought to use her closer proximity and take the blow so that he could grab her and disarm her quickly, but as she cut across the right of his torso, his roar of agony was far louder than it should have been.

His flesh sizzled where the knife pressed against it. I could see the steam rising into the air from it.

She knew enough to have a silver knife in her possession.

This little female was growing far more interesting by the second.

Lucas roared once more and his hands rushed to his side, trying to stem the flow of blood as he collapsed to the floor. She'd cut him deep. It probably wasn't a wound that would kill him, but with the coming fight he would be severely weakened.

Wounds made by silver weapons didn't heal like they were supposed to. I grimaced. I needed to protect my pack, not her.

"Shift, Lucas," I demanded. "Leave her to fight her own way."

He didn't even hesitate. At once, his body began to grow bigger, thick gray fur spurting out from beneath his skin. In a flurry of movement that took no more than a second, his spine expanded and crouched forward so that his paws met the floor. His teeth lengthened and his nails sharpened into thick claws. He roared as he shifted into his wolf form and he staggered under the pain of the injury the woman had inflicted, but it would be better for him this way. Silver knives were more effective in our human forms when we had nothing to protect us. In wolf form, however, our fur made it far more difficult to inflict that kind of injury. Plus, we shifted into an animal about the size of a bear. Our enemies were less likely to be able to get close enough to strike us in our wolf form.

The woman took a step back, probably trying to evaluate her strategy going forward. Her angry eyes met mine, her pretty little mouth set in a firm scowl. As much as I wanted to handle her myself, now was not the time for it. My pack needed me and as their alpha, I would never abandon them. She'd have to get out on her own.

"Good luck, human," I snarled, and I rushed into the fray just as the metal door we'd broken through slammed against the wall. A stream of vampires armed to the teeth rushed through the doors, many of them with rifles and a few of them with flamethrowers and even more with knives and pistols.

I would bet that all of them were armed with silver bullets.

Fuck. This was bad.

Just in time, Toboe's cell door slid open. Genzo had been able to hack it and Toboe raced out of it.

"Shift," I ordered my pack and they obeyed immediately. At once the room was full of massive red, gray, white, black, and brown wolves. I followed suit and in a rush, my sense of smell was stronger, my vision remarkably improved, and my hearing was heightened. Even in human form, my senses were quite strong, but in my wolf form they were truly extraordinary.

Our only true equals were vampires. Our wolf forms had evolved so that we could stand against them. A cocky wolf would think himself stronger than them, but that would be foolish.

Vampires were exceedingly fast and exceptionally strong. Their senses were just as heightened as ours. Different vampires were afforded various powerful abilities, including the charisma to force their human prey to do whatever they wanted, the skill to paralyze their prey, or the terrifying talent of causing them to go insane. The Venuti were strong, but they were fairly typical as far as vampire powers go. They could use their potent influence to make their human prey piss their pants in fear or fall in love with them even as they drained their blood. Their powers of persuasion were unmatched, but luckily that didn't affect us.

Their guns would though, especially if all of them were loaded with silver bullets. Getting through Venuti security was going to be a fight. In all likelihood, people were going to die from both sides.

My pack included.

"Be mindful of their guns. Do not underestimate them. Be smart. Our mission is to get out of here alive. Not to kill them all. Do you understand me?" I commanded. I didn't speak out loud, but the mental link between my pack members and me allowed us to communicate in silence even in the presence of our enemies.

A chorus of *"yes, alpha"* followed and in concert we branched out around the room. I didn't see any fully automatic weapons in our enemies' hands, but I wanted to err on the side of caution, nonetheless.

Slowly, the vampires and my pack circled each other. The head guard took a step forward and leveled a gun in my direction, but by the time he squeezed the trigger, I'd already moved far out of range of the shot. I bounded toward him, and he moved the gun to fire directly at me, but I had expected that. I feinted in one direction and caught him off guard before I closed my teeth around his wrist hard enough to shatter his bones to gristle and dust. The gun clattered down to the floor.

It wouldn't slow him down for long. I knew that.

The only ways to kill a vampire were sunlight, a stake through the heart, or the separation of their heads from their shoulders. They had several additional weaknesses, but none of those would be particularly useful to me right now.

The vampire faltered and I took advantage, lurching forward and capturing his throat in my teeth. I tasted blood as I bit through his throat, separating his head from his body in the process.

Vampires didn't have blood flowing through their veins. They didn't have a beating heart for that, which could only mean one thing. This one had fed recently.

Viciously, I jerked my head away and the vampire's head fell to the floor. The sickening sound of his cold body slapping against the floor echoed noisily. It took several seconds, but eventually his body began to wither away until the only thing left behind was a stinking dehydrated corpse.

I looked back, trying to see how the rest of my pack was faring. Not all of them had been as successful as I had been.

In despair, I watched as one of the vampires shot a silver bullet right in between Lucas' eyes. Having been injured by the human woman, his movements were slowed. His massive wolf form collapsed to the floor and slowly shifted back into the shape of a human.

The vampires had killed him, but there was no time for grief.

I looked around the room, only to see a few more of my men falling as they fought against the vampires. Some of my men were tearing through the vampires too, but from my cursory glance we were evenly matched.

"Run. Don't fight if you can manage it," I commanded.

I rushed at another vampire, trying to open a path for the rest of my pack to flee through. I bit down on his wrist and threw him aside into the wall, but the bastard landed like a spider and flew back toward me with wild abandon. I rolled out of the way just before he landed on me. He reached for a gun on his belt. I bit his hand clean off. That would grow back, but it would take a minute or two. He snarled in response and circled me. I growled right back at him.

In a flurry of motion, I rushed at him, using my massive form to knock him aside once again. A few of my pack members made it to the door and out into the hall, but there were still too many of them left behind me for me to make my way out.

I fought tooth and nail so that as many of them could get out as they could. Toboe's massive gray form finally bounded to my side, and he grunted as a single silver bullet grazed his right shoulder. He didn't let it slow him down even though I knew it hurt.

As the alpha, I was the largest and strongest wolf. As my beta, Toboe was my second in command and his size and strength followed suit. We were the only two with a definitive edge over these guards. The silver bullets made even that difference difficult though.

I tore through several vampires before all my remaining men were able to make it out the door. By the time that happened, I'd already lost six of my men. Just as Toboe and I were about to exit the room, something strange happened.

The human woman flew into the midst of the battle just as all of us were about to make a run for it.

I snarled, wanting to jump back in and carry her out myself, but then she pulled a sleek-looking little gun from God knows where.

Impressive. Apparently she'd smuggled that in too.

She leveled the gun at the vampire closest to her and he laughed. She pulled the trigger at almost point-blank range and I watched as a gold bullet burst forth. He let it hit him right between the eyes, fully expecting it to bounce off his forehead.

It didn't. It pierced right through his unnaturally hard vampire skin.

I saw the wound for a split second before a blinding, extremely powerful white light burst forth from within him. It was as bright as the sun and the vampire's head exploded in a violent display of light. He'd probably fed recently too because an alarming amount of blood and gore splattered all over the place. The body of the vampire collapsed to the floor, headless and entirely motionless. He wouldn't come back from that. She shot another before she burst toward the door and sprinted down the hallway herself. I watched her go before I bounded out in the hallway to follow my men.

Well, wasn't that something. I'd never seen anything like it. I'd never even heard of anything that powerful that would take out a vampire. Ever.

And she'd taken out two of them. A human.

I sprinted after her with Toboe at my side.

At first, she raced in the same direction as we did. Silver bullets peppered the floor as the remaining vampires raced after us, but a lot of them missed, ricocheting off the walls and the floor behind us. One grazed my ear and I bit back a snarl of agony as it burned away at my flesh, but I didn't slow down. I expected her to go the same direction, but when the time came for me to turn into the vault, she kept running past it.

I couldn't go after her. I had to make sure that my pack made it out alive.

I swerved into the room and pulled back just enough for Toboe to dive through the hole first. I quickly followed suit and tore out into the tunnel with the rest of my men.

"Now, Genzo!" I roared.

I watched as he rushed forward and slammed his paws on top of the platform ignition that he'd set up in the event that we were followed in our hasty retreat out of this place.

The earth rumbled beneath our feet. I sprinted out of the tunnel after my pack, and behind me the world exploded into an elegant display of fire and dust.

There was one more way to kill a vampire. They couldn't put themselves back together if you blew them to smithereens.

As I ran out of the tunnel to join my remaining pack members, I wasn't thinking about those I lost. Instead, my mind was embroiled with thoughts of the tiny human woman who had not only injured one of my wolf shifter brethren, she'd also killed two vampires with some kind of exploding light bullets.

I couldn't stop thinking about it. Why would a human have access to something like that and why would she be held prisoner by the vampires when she could kill them as she pleased?

I wanted to know more. I needed to know more.

She'd gotten away from me today, but I had her scent now. The only thing I had to do now was follow it. I'd find her and she would tell me what I wanted to know.

As much as I wanted to deny it, I had a feeling this wouldn't be the last time I broke into the Venuti tower, and it most certainly wouldn't be the last time I had to deal with the Venuti themselves.

Although…

If I was able to get my hands on that woman's weapon… that might change things. That could tip the odds in our favor in a major way.

She could run, hide, and fight me all she wanted. I was going to find her, and I was going to get some answers.

CHAPTER 2

*A*va

A week later

My life had turned into a nightmare, one that was constantly plagued with long bouts of insomnia and terrible dreams.

I don't remember the last time I'd gotten a full night's sleep. It had been weeks. Maybe even months because every time I lay down and closed my eyes, I saw my father's last moments play out in my mind, over and over again for the world to see until the end of time.

Forever captured on video.

Forever a murderer.

My family would carry the stigma of it forever.

The gunshots echoed in my head, and I groaned with annoyance, pressing my face into the white cotton pillow beneath it. I squeezed my eyes shut and tried to think of anything but the crazed look in his eyes as that fateful scene ran across my mind for the nine billionth time.

But it wouldn't stop.

It never stopped.

Ever.

It had been a massacre. My father had walked into Café Du Monde, where tourists and locals alike were enjoying a coffee in the late morning with the powdery sugar-loaded beignets that they were so famous for and pulled out a submachine gun.

The person who had captured it all on film had been a traveling college student from England, a young man who'd been inordinately excited about trying the sugary pastries he'd seen on several videos on YouTube. He'd brought his high school sweetheart to New Orleans with them, and he'd planned to propose that night at a fancy dinner at a steakhouse in the French Quarter.

I could still hear his voice like he was sitting there in the room with me, asking his girl if she wanted a coffee with her beignets. She smiled at him, her eyes sparkling with excitement of visiting America for the first time. She'd nodded with enthusiasm, looking forward to her breakfast just as much as he was.

I'd never forget the way her smile faltered as she looked over his shoulder, the camera still facing her and the way her mouth suddenly twisted in raw fear. Everything went insane after that. The video flew back and forth as they rushed to hide beneath the table, taking cover on the floor amidst the powdered sugar and dirt beneath them.

The camera had panned back, and the shooting had started. In fear, the young man had dropped his equipment, but not before it captured the face of my father on film.

There'd been no doubt that it was him. None.

They called it a mental break of some kind, that he'd been fine one day and had just snapped the next, but that wasn't enough for me. The people who had made that diagnosis had never even met him. They hadn't known anything about him aside from the files that had been prepared about him.

I'd seen them.

They'd all been a lie. Every word.

Right up to the moment that a group of men had surrounded him and broken his neck in the middle of the busiest café in the French Quarter.

The file had said they were cops, but I knew better. I knew what they were.

They were vampires.

I knew because my father had told me about them.

I knew the man behind the monster the media had painted him to be.

My dad had been sweet and caring. Years ago, he'd been a respected professor at the University of Louisiana. He'd taught mechanical engineering for years, but he'd stepped away from that in order to take a position as a consultant for a small company before he branched out on his own. Taking control of his career had been far more lucrative, yet it brought a certain set of dangers along with it.

His clients were dangerous, sometimes crime families, sometimes monsters, sometimes both. Some of them were shifters. Others were vampires. There were more, but he didn't tell me about them all. He'd taught me to protect myself against them nonetheless, ever since I was a little girl. I grew up knowing that much of the world was run by the hands of monsters. I'd done my best to avoid them all my life, but then it had turned personal when they'd somehow turned my father into the villain that shot up Café Du Monde.

My father had never been a killer. I was convinced there was something more behind his death. I was sure of it.

Before he was killed, he'd started meeting with a new batch of clients. I'd known only the bare minimum in that they were members of the Venuti Clan, but he hadn't told me what for or why, but I did know he'd taken a job with monsters and ended up dead.

I couldn't accept what they said on the news. My father hadn't been mentally ill. He hadn't lost his sanity. He hadn't decided to end it all.

No. I would never accept any of that. I couldn't. I know he didn't just snap. I needed to know who did that to him.

I needed to clear my family's name.

What if the reason he broke was vampires? What if it had been the Venuti that had compelled him to act that way? What if they'd taken away his will and forced him to murder helpless innocents? I needed to know the reason.

I'd sacrifice everything to find those answers.

Honestly, I didn't care if I wound up dead. I needed to know.

All I knew was that it had something to do with my father's sunfire bullets.

He'd explained the science of them to me once. They had a solid magnesium ribbon inside the core. Once the gun was fired, it exposed the magnesium to oxygen and *boom*. An explosion of light and heat that could rival sunlight. The perfect weapon for killing vampires.

It was a secret he'd shared with me just days before he died. He'd taught me how to make them because he wanted to keep me safe.

With a sigh, I opened my eyes and stared at the ceiling. I was lucky if I slept more than three hours since I'd gone to bed somewhere around midnight. The full moon shone through the maple leaves of the tree outside my window, sending my room into a flickering showcase of light and shadow. It was really quite pretty, and on a normal night I might have enjoyed it.

But… something was different. Something felt off.

The hair on the back of my neck rose and I felt the sudden sensation that I was no longer alone in my own room. Someone was here in my room with me.

I'd learned to trust my gut a long time ago and this time would be no different.

With a nervous swallow, I pushed my hands against the bed so I could sit against my headboard. As my upper back pressed against the padded leather surface, my gaze passed around the room to the soft recliner I had beside the window. I had initially set it up as my own personal reading nook, but the gray fabric chair was currently occupied by a very large man in a very nice suit. The light of the moon was just enough to illuminate him in shadow, but I could see enough of him to know that I'd come across him somewhere before.

I tried to rack my brain for any reason why and how a man like him would be sitting here in my room.

In a perfect world, he would be a male model. His hair was dark gold, a perfect mix of mahogany and golden threads, a beautiful color that reminded me of a sandy beach after a sudden rainstorm. It was full and thick, and long enough for me to run my fingers through and grab just enough to pull his head back by it. His jawline was covered by a thick beard that was neat and trim and the sudden urge to feel the scrape of it against my skin passed through me.

I swallowed hard, annoyed at myself for thinking something like that.

It was obvious that he was well off. I wasn't certain of the maker of his suit in the dark, but it was either Saint Laurent or Valentino by the look of it. It was very fine black material with a hint of dark gray shimmer that happened to catch the moonlight perfectly. A pristinely white button-up shirt was beneath it. His tie was perfectly done, the fabric covered in a silvery gray rectangular pattern that shone like silk, which it probably was. His matching slacks were flawlessly pressed, and his black leather shoes looked like they had been recently buffed and shined.

Everything about him spoke of money, but more than that, it spoke to his power.

His gaze bored into mine, sparkling with a certain amusement and an even harder edge hinting at a deeper darkness that should have scared me. His irises were hazel, a captivating mixture of emerald and browns and yellows. The colors only seemed to intensify under the light of the moon and as the branches shifted outside my window, they began to change. In the shadows, they appeared to be greener, and, in the light, the yellow hue burned bright enough to shine like gold.

He was a wolf shifter.

He'd been the one to break open my cage in the Venuti tower. He'd been the one who had given me back my freedom and now he was sitting here in my room.

I knew enough about him from that night to know that he was dangerous. I'd need to protect myself from whatever this was.

I lifted my chin, pressing my lips firmly together and tensing hard. I didn't look, but I prepared myself to grab the silver knife on my bedside table. I always kept it there beside a wooden stake just in case of times like this.

"Ava Winters," he breathed, and I stiffened.

He knew my name...

"I know all about your recent adventures, little human. I'm here to ask you some questions and you're going to answer. If you cooperate, I will leave you here in peace. If not, I'm going to have to punish you for your disobedience," he purred, and I decided I didn't like the way goosebumps were rising all over my arms just at the sound of his voice. I pressed my thighs together anxiously and prepared myself to fight.

As if they offered some kind of protection, I pulled the covers up to my chest, using the thick quilts to cover the hard buds of my nipples that were probably mortifyingly obvious beneath the thin fabric of my cotton nightgown.

One of the straps slid down my arm and I rushed to put it back into place, oddly bothered by the fact that he could see the bareness of my shoulder.

I felt my face heat with embarrassment.

It was just my luck that he'd catch me in this nightgown. The straps never seemed to stay up, no matter if I tightened them or not. I'd been meaning to get something new for forever, but I'd never gotten around to it.

I was going to throw it out tomorrow for sure.

"I want to know about the weapon you used against the vampires. The gun appeared to be factory standard, but the bullets you used certainly weren't," he said.

I gritted my teeth and decided that it was time to act.

Without even a second of hesitation, I reached for my bedside table while keeping my eyes trained on him. My fingers brushed against the wooden surface, and I froze. Nothing. A flicker of panic raced through me, and I looked quickly, finding both the knife and the stake gone.

Shit.

Immediately, I turned back to him as he cleared his throat.

"Is this what you were reaching for?" he asked expectantly, and my gaze tore to his fingers. He was holding the knife by the handle, very carefully avoiding the silver blade with his grasp. I snarled and threw the covers off me, racing toward my bedroom door. My bare feet dug into the carpet, but as quickly as I moved, I knew he would be faster.

I gave it all I had anyway. The work my father had done was dangerous, so he had ensured that I'd had access to all the trainers I could ever need. I'd studied with some of the most renowned teachers, learning all aspects of various fighting techniques throughout the world. You name it, I studied it. If he caught me, I would use everything I'd ever learned to make sure he let me go and I got away.

I only just made it to the entryway of my bedroom before his arms circled around my waist. I screeched and grasped at the doorframe, trying to use brute force to break his hold on me.

It didn't work.

As if I weighed no more than a bag of feathers, he tossed me on the bed. I tried to push myself back up, lurching toward the door once more. He was too fast for that. It was as if he was ready for every move I made.

In a flurry of movement, he pushed me ruthlessly hard down on the bed on my back with just the force of his hand. Unexpectedly, he climbed over top of me and sat astride me with his knees on either side of my waist. I tried to bring my knee up behind him, but he clicked his tongue in disapproval.

"I had hoped you'd make this difficult," he murmured. Immediately, I tried to pry my way out from under him. This was fight or flight and right now, I just wanted to escape.

"Let me go," I demanded. I pounded my fists against his chest, and he brushed my hands aside like I was nothing more than a fly.

"I told you how this was going to go, Ava."

I pushed against the firmness of his chest, trying to squirm out from underneath him. His muscles rippled underneath my palms, giving away just how hard he was beneath his shirt. Without delay, he pushed my hands once more to the side as if they weren't there at all and then unbuttoned the top of his suit jacket. He shrugged it off and tossed it to the side. As the shadows flickered across his chest, I could see almost every ridge of muscle through the pressed white cotton of his button-up shirt, the broad set of his shoulders, the toned lines of his stomach, and the rippling bulge of his pecs.

It was at that moment that I became aware of something else.

My pussy was wet.

And not just a little.

A whole lot.

To this date, I'd never been bested by anyone, human or monster. I'd always been able to fight my way out of anything. Hell, I'd fought my way out of the Venuti tower and killed at least a dozen vampires along the way.

This man had singlehandedly manhandled me into a position that I couldn't figure out a way to get out of and that was so terrifying that my body was reacting of its own accord. Much to my irritation, my clit pulsed with arousal at the thought.

What the hell was wrong with me?

He stared down at me, his eyes dark with cruel intention.

"Such a tiny human, but so much fire," he breathed. He reached for me, and I flinched as he brushed a lock of hair off my forehead back behind my ear. He chuckled at my reaction, dragging his fingertips across my cheek and down along my jawline. Then he pressed a single finger firmly down the line of my throat. He followed the ridge of my collarbone until he reached the thick strap of my nightgown and slipped his fingers just underneath it.

His touch was hot against my skin, practically setting me aflame, and I hated it. I pressed my thighs firmly together as he studied me underneath him, trying to use sheer will to push away the rising arousal that seemed to be running rampant from somewhere deep inside me.

It didn't work and I detested that he appeared to notice my discomfort.

"I think I'm going to enjoy this very much," he murmured, his words carrying a dark undertone that sent a shiver racing down my spine at the same time that my pussy felt like it was catching fire.

He took hold of the strap more firmly now. With no warning, he tore it clean off as if he was simply ripping a piece of paper. Systematically, he did the same to the other side. With one hand, he captured my wrists and I tried to pull away, but he was so much stronger than me and with barely any effort on his part, he reached over my head and tied my right arm to the bedpost. With measured swiftness, he did the same to the other side and when he was done, he paused and stared down into my eyes.

As if he was letting my captivity really sink in.

He was the predator, and I was his prey. He was bigger, faster, stronger, and superior in every way.

I tested the bonds gingerly at first and they held fast. I tried harder and I still couldn't get free. I twisted and turned my hands, pulling against them as firmly as I could.

I couldn't get out. I was his prisoner, his captive to do with as he wished.

This was bad.

He reached for me again, but this time his fingertips grazed along the sweetheart neckline of my nightgown. I gasped in fear, but it came out sounding more wanton than I wanted it to. The edges of his mouth perked up in a smirk and then it was gone, as if it had never been there in the first place.

"You're not wearing a bra, Ava. Do you know how I know that?" he asked, and I gritted my teeth.

"Fuck off," I spat. He wasn't going to get me to admit anything, especially when it concerned my very aroused and traitorous body. I'd hide that no matter what.

"It's such a simple design. Thin cotton decorated with light pink embroidery, but it does nothing to hide how very hard your nipples are beneath the fabric. If the lights were on, I bet it would be sheer enough so that I could see the outline of your areolas, wouldn't I?"

I didn't answer him because he was right.

The fabric was more than a little worn through from the wash. Why couldn't I have worn something else tonight?

But it turned out that I didn't have to say anything at all because he grasped the neckline of my nightgown and tore it right open, baring my breasts in less time than it took me to draw in another breath.

"You bastard!" I screeched.

"I'll tell you a secret, little human. Even in the dim light of the moon, I can still see them. My eyesight is especially good, even more so in the dark. One of the perks of being a wolf," he said.

"Fuck. You," I answered and I spat right in his face. For a moment, he stilled, and I watched my spittle drip down his cheek. I expected anger, but his gaze remained steady and calm.

"Bad girl. You're going to pay for that."

With ruthless intention, he grasped my nipples between his thumbs and forefingers. For a second, he just held them in his clutches before he pinched them hard. If I had expected gentleness or mercy of any kind, I would have been sorely disappointed.

A cry of pain escaped my lips before I could stop it.

A vicious flare of agony blossomed from the tips of my nipples, radiating downward and spreading with electrifying intensity until it centered in the depths of my core. He twisted them hard, and I keened with fright, embroiled in wave after wave of punishing pain that left me feeling helpless and afraid and undoubtedly angry.

He squeezed harder and I started to panic before he finally released them. The wave of agony that followed was almost as intense as it was initially, but it eventually ebbed away to a gentler aching throb long after he let them go.

I trembled beneath him, feeling real fear for the first time.

For a long time, he stared down at my breasts. The pads of his fingers grazed over top of my sore nipples, reawakening the hurt he'd forced upon them. I didn't say anything more, too shell-shocked to do anything but lie there trapped beneath him.

He leaned forward, just grazing his lips against my ear. I gasped as his breath tickled the tiny hairs along my skin and I desperately tried to ignore how it was causing little bolts of electricity to trickle down so far that my clit started with pulse with it.

I wanted my body to stop reacting to him. I didn't want to enjoy his threats or the way his touch was making me tremble with shameful need. I didn't want any of it.

"I want you to think about something, Ava," he whispered, and the rumble of his words made me clutch my thighs together as if that could protect me from whatever was to come.

At least I was wearing panties. I thanked God that I had decided to put on a pair tonight.

I didn't respond because I was afraid my voice would give away everything that was running through my head.

"I want you to think about the fact that you'll be telling me everything I want to know one way or another, but I'm *very* much looking forward to punishing you for your refusal to do so in the first place. You should know that in the end you're going to beg to be allowed to tell me what I want to know and then, just maybe, I'll finish your punishment in the way it would please me the most before I finally give you permission to tell me what I want to know," he whispered in my ear, his words tickling me in a way that made my pussy clench with burning need.

I shouldn't want to fuck him.

I should want to kill him. I should want to use my silver knife to stab him right in the fucking heart.

"I'm not going to tell you anything," I snarled.

I could feel his lips curling up in a smile against my ear. He was enjoying my defiance and I didn't know if that bode well for me. For all I knew, it was just making things worse.

But he was a monster. He was a thing I could never trust.

"Do you think you're in control, little human?" he asked, and I jerked my wrists in an effort to break my bonds once more. He chuckled and an ice-cold chill hurtled through my veins, sinking right down into the marrow of my bones.

"Who are you?" I spat.

"My name is Lawson Clearwater. I'm the alpha of the Crescent Moon Pack," he answered.

I froze.

Everything started to make way more sense. He was the kingpin of the Crescent Moon Pack, the *alpha*. He headed the biggest wolf family here in New Orleans, which was really only opposed by the Venuti vampire clan. Very few people knew of their existence because they liked it that way, but they were far more powerful than any human mafia families here in the city. If either the Crescent Moon Pack or the Venuti Clan decided to eliminate the Gambinos or the Genovese family that reigned down here too, they could do it in less than twenty-four hours.

"Have you ever tried to fight off an alpha before, little human?" he purred.

I shook my head, glaring at him as he drew back just enough to stare into my eyes. His irises sparkled like yellow diamonds. The emerald had lightened to something of a peridot color, hidden behind the golden yellow that gave away his real identity. His gaze was like looking into stained glass, but with far more power behind it. I found myself getting lost inside his eyes before I forced myself to turn away.

"Let me go, you mangy bastard," I growled, and he laughed openly before he leaned down low enough to brush his lips against my nipples.

"Get off! What are you doing?" I yelled.

"Such a bad, bad girl. It's time you began to understand what a punishment by my hands means," he murmured.

There was no time to prepare for what came next. I couldn't have, even if I'd tried and not even if he warned me with what he was about to do.

He pulled back his lips with a snarl and used his teeth to capture my right nipple. He bit down hard, and I shrieked as the pain from before rushed back and escalated to something far beyond just the pinching of his fingers.

My nipple felt scalded by his harshness, and I tried to breathe through it, but his teeth pressed more firmly around it and I couldn't stop myself from crying out.

The agony intensified, building higher and higher until it radiated across my entire breast, sinking deep into my body with every passing wave of it. I tried to pull away, but that only made it hurt more, made the pain run deeper. Instead, I arched my back and tried to press into his bite, but he pulled away with my nipple still firmly locked in between his teeth.

"Please! Please!" I cried out. The words flew from my lips before I could stop them. This hurt so very much, and I just wanted him to let go. I keened and closed my eyes, trying to stop myself from crying from just how much it hurt.

My nipples had always been especially sensitive.

Finally, he opened his lips and I fell back against the bed, blinking away the hot tears that were threatening to fall. My nipple throbbed hot, and I looked down, fearful that he had marked it, but there was nothing more than just an impression left behind from his teeth.

His mouth moved to the left side, and I panicked.

"Please! Don't!" I begged. His tongue slipped out from between his lips and curled up, just licking the tip of my nipple with gentle promise.

"You don't know me well enough yet, little girl, but you should know that it isn't up to you. I will deal with you however I please. It will never matter how much you beg," he warned.

He bit my left nipple after that. I don't know if it was as hard or harder than the right side, but it felt worse maybe because I knew what was coming. I knew it was going to hurt, but experiencing it was something else altogether.

I thrashed beneath him, desperate to escape but it did nothing. He held my nipple between his teeth, tightening as hard as he wished until at long last, he released me.

I panted hard, trying to grapple with the pain as it gradually faded away. It throbbed with continual hurt, tiny aftershocks of soreness that refused to ebb long after he was through with punishing me there.

"I enjoy seeing my teeth marks on your pretty little nipples, but they aren't pink enough for me yet. I'm going to have to make sure they're spanked properly after I tear the rest of your nightgown off," he threatened.

What?

He took advantage of my momentary confusion to shift backwards so that his body was situated just over my thighs.

I still couldn't move enough to buck him off of me, not that I could even hope to throw a man of his massive size.

He probably weighed twice what I did. At least.

He wasted no time in gripping the fabric of my nightgown and tearing right through it. It fell apart in his fingers as if it was nothing but a pile of threads, baring the rest of me in a matter of seconds.

I sucked in a nervous breath. The fabric scraped against my punished nipples as he pulled it away, and I whimpered softly as the ache from before intensified into a hard throb.

His palm cradled my left breast tenderly. I stilled, trying to study his face for any hint as to his plans. I saw nothing. Not even a hint of malice or anything else before the touch of his fingers faded away only to return with brutal force.

He smacked my breast, and I could only just watch as the marks from his fingers flared white and then bright pink, stark against the paleness of my skin. He did it again. And again.

I thrashed beneath him, trying to avoid his palm, yet still his aim was true every time. He spanked all over my breasts and just when I thought it couldn't get any worse, he held me in place and smacked my nipple directly. He focused on one side and then the other and just when I thought I would break and scream, he stopped and sucked in an appreciative breath.

"There now. Your pretty breasts are so beautiful when they've been spanked bright pink," he mused.

He sat back and gazed over my bared body, admiring the handiwork of his mark on my skin. He stared at me for what felt like forever, letting his eyes linger on the fullness of my breasts and the gentle curve of my waist before it dipped even lower to study the light blue lace trim of my silky panties.

"You will ask me to remove your panties, Ava. Ask me to show you just how wet they already are," he coaxed firmly, and I shook my head.

I couldn't ask him to do that. I wouldn't.

"No," I scoffed. "I'd never ask that of the likes of you."

I couldn't live with myself if I did.

"Do you think you can hide your arousal from me, little human?" he asked carefully.

"I'm not aroused," I snapped. I'd never admit something like that, especially to him.

"Yes, you are, little one. Not only can I see your wetness seeping through the seat of your panties, but I can smell it. An alpha like me can sense it by the scent alone," he murmured, and I gave one last-ditch effort to try to buck him off. I did it even though I knew I'd fail.

He laughed openly this time, and the effect was chilling.

His fingers grazed along the lacy hem of my panties, glancing just beneath it to brush against my skin. His touch was gentle at first, just gliding back and forth. It was strangely calming initially, pulling me into a gentle lull that maybe the worst was over for at least a little while.

That didn't last very long.

He slipped his hand just far enough underneath my panties before he curled his fingers and grasped them firmly enough to hurt just the slightest bit. I jerked away as he pulled them tight enough to wedge the fabric between my wet and sensitive folds.

He held still for a moment, and I froze.

"What are you doing?" I asked nervously, my voice beginning to shake and reveal just how anxious I was beneath him. I hated myself for not being able to hide that.

He said nothing and simply jerked my panties harder against me, capturing my clit beneath them. Then he relaxed his hold just a little before pulling them up against me once again. The fabric of my panties rubbed against my clit roughly as he repeated the motion over and over.

The cloth burned. At first it was painfully jarring, and I struggled to think of anything more I could do to get him to stop. I'd run out of options. There was no getting out of this.

For the first time in my life, I was completely helpless. This man, this perfect stranger, could do whatever he wanted to me, and I wouldn't be able to stop him.

Any woman in her right mind would have been terrified.

But not me.

Apparently, that thought in particular just made me wetter and even more aroused than before and now the fabric of my panties was rubbing against my clit and forcing me to face things I didn't want to.

Forcing me to recognize my arousal.

Forcing me to admit the truth.

I wanted to come. Badly. With the hands of an alpha on my bare flesh.

The fabric moved faster and the orgasm I wanted to push away so badly raged forth. I tried to think of anything to keep it at bay, but nothing worked. I thought about the fact that he was a wolf shifter, but that only seemed to escalate the rising heat between my thighs. He was a monster, a criminal, but right now he was so focused on forcing my release that nothing could stop my orgasm from breaking over me like a sudden storm.

His movements were so rough that my clit burned red hot. Even though it was painful, the arousal in my core only seemed to clench tighter. At some point, it started to become far more pleasurable than I expected, molding together with the pain and becoming something far stronger altogether.

His movements were so rough, so different than the gentle feeling of my own fingers between my thighs.

I'd never felt the touch of a man there before him. Ever.

Held captive, I drowned in the roughness of it. There was nothing gentle about the way he rubbed my clit with my panties. He forced my pleasure forth and before long, I felt like I was tiptoeing on the edge of a cliff about to fall off at any moment.

I moaned out loud for the first time.

"You're going to come for me, little human. I'm not going to give you a choice," he warned, and my nipples throbbed hot just as I arched into the growing sensation between my thighs.

"Please don't!" I yelped. Even as I said the words, I was unsure if I actually wanted more, for him to be rougher, or if I really wanted him to stop.

Fuck.

It only got more intense after that.

Just when I thought he couldn't get any rougher, he did. He rubbed my clit with ruthless obsession, forcing my orgasm whether I wanted it or not.

But I did.

I was going to come. Hard.

With my clit burning from the constantly rubbing cloth of my panties, I fell off that edge into the strongest orgasm I'd ever had in my life. My own fingers paled in comparison. Even my little egg-shaped bullet vibrator couldn't hold a candle to this single forced orgasm at the hands of an alpha wolf.

With a pitiful cry, I arched upward just as my thighs began to tremble. I fell deep into the blissful chasm of mind-rending pleasure. I closed my eyes, the light of the moon becoming far too bright to behold, but that wasn't all I was hiding from.

I didn't want to see the look of victory in his eyes when he saw what I looked like when I came for him.

My orgasm went on longer than it ever had before. My core twisted tight, and my clit pulsed with scalding hot sensation. My pussy clenched down hard, my inner walls fluttering with need.

I felt so empty.

I wanted to feel him inside me.

I'd played with a dildo before all by myself in a dark room. I blushed at the vision of what it might have looked like when I fucked myself with that toy.

All of a sudden, I felt the need to take his cock deep inside me. I was so needy that I lost focus of everything else entirely.

My thighs continued to tremble as my release went on and just when it reached its peak, my eyes rolled back in my head.

My orgasms had always been quiet. I'd never been a screamer.

Until now.

Until him.

I lost control and I writhed, screaming my pleasure along with it. White fiery ecstasy pulsed through me and when it finally released me from its wondrous captivity, I was left panting and breathless and utterly exhausted.

Oh, fuck.

That felt good.

"You will ask me to take off your panties, little one," he demanded.

Wait. What?

I blinked, still caught in the flowery haze of bliss of that orgasm. Even though my clit throbbed with both pain and pleasure, it wasn't enough to make me ask for something so shameful.

I shook my head.

"No," I whispered, my voice hoarse from screaming.

His other hand worked between my thighs, dipping down to my entrance. Very slowly, he pressed two fingers inside me, carefully keeping the fabric of my panties snugly pinched between them.

I cried out, so caught off guard to suddenly feel his fingers inside my pussy. I hated that it felt so insanely good.

"This little pussy is so very tight. Tell me, am I the first man to touch it?"

I flushed hard. He didn't need to know I was a virgin. I was twenty-five, but I'd never had time for a man or the patience for one. Men my age were immature, obsessed with partying and getting with as many girls as humanly possible. That hadn't been enough to hold my interest, so I'd never sought one out.

Lawson grinned with conquest.

"I thought so," he murmured knowingly, and I blanched as his fingers slid inside me even deeper. I cried out as he slowly pushed into me, his fingers feeling far larger than the one toy I'd been brave enough to play with in the privacy of my own bedroom.

"As punishment, my bad little girl, you're going to come for me again," he threatened.

"I can't," I squeaked.

I'd never come more than once in my life. I'd attempted it just once and my clit had been far too sensitive to the touch to even dare it. I'd given up almost as soon as I had started.

"Do you think it's up to you, naughty girl?"

He began to fuck me roughly with his thick fingers, using his other hand to jerk my panties back and forth. When he placed a thumb over top of the fabric that covered my clit, I knew I was lost.

I cried out as that familiar painful sensation returned, but this time I couldn't escape it. This time it wasn't my own fingers in charge, but his.

My inner walls clutched greedily at his fingers, either wanting them deeper or needing to push them out. My nipples hardened even more than I thought possible, aching and pulsing from his punishing bite still. My nostrils flared as I tried to draw in air and my heart pounded in my chest.

The agony between my legs only grew more intense. This time, the pain far outweighed the pleasure. When I would have stopped, he pushed past it and just when it felt like it was too much to bear, my body relented, and I shattered.

I thought I'd come hard the first time.

The second one devastated me.

His fingers moved roughly between my thighs, and I felt every ridge, every knuckle, every inch of friction from the thickness of those masterful digits. He fucked me with them hard. He wasn't gentle and they hurt too. My pussy couldn't seem to get used to the girth of those fingers and it burned hot as they constantly stretched me open. The cloth fabric of my soaked panties still roughly rubbed against my clit, and I couldn't hold off the onslaught of pleasure even if I'd tried.

I screamed from the very beginning. My legs shook and I tried to close them, but it didn't matter. He jerked the fabric so much harder, so much more roughly, and I responded with far more intensity than I could have ever prepared for.

My throat started to grow hoarse, but the drowning abyss of my release continued. This orgasm felt as if a knife was twisting deep in my core, threatening to tear me open and render me entirely defenseless and utterly wrecked.

"Oh, please!" I screamed, my pussy clamping down around his fingers like a vise. My body held him firmly, but still he pushed past that tightness and fucked me with those fingers hard enough that I knew I would be sore long after he was through with me.

My release lasted far longer than I thought it would and when it finally started to fade away, I was left a whimpering mess of well-satisfied woman. My body slumped into the bed, all fight drained away and I just focused on the effort it took to draw one breath after another into my lungs.

I'd come two times in a row.

I closed my eyes, just trying to calm down. My heart pounded in my chest so hard that I thought it would fly right out. My blood rushed so swiftly through my veins that it sounded like a surging river in my head.

I was worn out. I hadn't been able to sleep before, but I was certain that I would be able to now. I'd be able to sleep like a goddamn baby. I was that tired.

"I'm going to give you one last chance, bad girl. Ask me to remove your panties."

CHAPTER 3

Ava

He couldn't mean that. He couldn't. I told myself that over and over because I was in unknown territory. If I refused, would he make me come again? Would he leave? Would he do something else?

Did he want to fuck me?

Did I want him to?

I swallowed hard and met his eyes. At once, all the questions in my mind fell away. He was dead serious. I'd never been so certain of anything in my life.

I was exhausted. My pussy was sore. My clit and my nipples throbbed hot.

But I still had my pride. It was all I had left.

I shook my head, refusing him for a third time. I would never ask for him to remove my panties. I wouldn't be a willing participant in whatever this was.

Not now. Not ever.

His mouth set in a firm line and without missing a beat, he pulled his fingers from my pussy and tore my panties clean off. The fabric caught my sensitive folds, ripping against my aching clit and burning hot like a brand. I cried out, feeling as though he'd scraped my flesh from my body. I blinked hard, trying to rein back the tears that suddenly threatened to fall. My pussy ached long after he tore my panties from me, a powerful reminder of just how strong he was.

Fire.

Oh, God.

It hurt.

My clit wouldn't stop burning.

I couldn't stop screaming so he took my soaked panties and stuffed them in my mouth, effectively gagging me with them. The taste of my own arousal washed across my tongue, sweet and musky and shamefully arousing. I felt myself blush with embarrassment, blazing even hotter when I saw his gaze dip downward to take in the sight between my legs.

His fingers curled around my pussy, and he met my eyes with his hard unforgiving ones.

"Bad girl. I gave you three chances and still, you refuse me. I wasn't planning on spanking this naughty little pussy tonight, but you most certainly earned it," he growled.

I cried out into the soaked cloth of my panties in fear.

If he hadn't cut off my ability to speak, I would have begged him not to. I had the feeling it wouldn't have mattered though. He'd have done it anyway.

The first time his palm slapped against the overly sensitive flesh of my pussy, I screeched around the sodden cloth in my mouth as a rush of fierce agony spread across my wet folds. His hand was fast and hard, striking against my bare flesh with ruthless and terrible intent.

This was a punishment. This hurt a lot and there was no way for me to make it stop. My only choice was to take all of it until he decided that he had given me enough. I wailed in despair.

I tried to close my legs in a protective measure, but he shifted once more and placed a single knee between my thighs, keeping me vulnerable and open to his punishing hand. Over and over, he spanked my pussy, thoroughly punishing my tender flesh as hard as he wanted.

Then he used his fingers to spread my pussy wide open, baring my clit. He spanked that next. I thrashed and writhed as much as I could, but it all was for naught. I squeezed my eyes shut, willing myself not to break.

The last thing I wanted was for him to see me cry.

"I'm sorry," I screamed into my soaked panties, but he didn't listen, and I was left to suffer with the taste of my wetness on my tongue and the burning sting of his punishing hand between my thighs.

"Are you ready to tell me where you got the weapon you used to kill the vampires?" he pressed.

I shook my head, trying to tell him to stop and that I desperately wanted him to stop spanking my pussy so brutally hard.

He was a monster. I couldn't tell him anything.

Even if I wanted this all to stop.

His mouth set in a firm line and his gaze darkened. He held my pussy open and spanked my clit several times in quick succession and then he pinched it so hard that I swore that I saw stars.

I cried out in pain and reluctant pleasure. My pussy felt scalded from his punishment, but still my desire for more seemed to rise from the fire as if it was immortal, and nothing I could do would bring it down.

I didn't know how it was possible, but I was coming to the terrifying conclusion that he could force me to come for a third time.

I didn't know if I could take it. I didn't even know if I was capable of it.

"You will beg to tell me what I want to know," he warned and the veiled threat in his tone that he could do far more to me if he wanted to was so terrifying that I stilled with fright.

There wasn't any doubt in my mind that he would.

But I couldn't give in. With fear, I shook my head. I refused him once more because I had no other choice.

He shifted backwards once more, holding down my legs with the strength of his arms as he lowered his mouth to my pussy. He blew a warm breath over top of my scalded flesh, and I shivered.

"I bit your nipples as punishment earlier, didn't I little one?" he asked purposefully.

I nodded.

"Your little clit can suffer the same fate," he warned, and I tried to jerk away in an ill-conceived escape attempt.

I keened into the gag in my mouth as he opened his lips and I watched in open horror as his teeth moved forward and latched around my clit.

For a second, he held my clit just so with his teeth. I shook with panic, unable to do anything but sit there and look on in disbelief before he bit down on my tender bud so roughly and cruelly that the punishing hurt was agony from the first moment.

I cried out before the pain even began. My clit was more than overly sensitive from the two forced orgasms at his hands, and he probably knew it. Pure pain and exquisite pleasure poured through me, two warring sensations and before long, the hurtful edge began to win out. I screamed and I cried out. I begged through the sodden cloth of my panties and when he finally released my clit, I moaned in sheer relief even as it continued to throb with punishing soreness.

As the pain began to fade, I was left with something even more powerful.

Desire.

The unfathomable need for more.

I wanted him to fuck me, and I wanted it badly. I wanted to feel his cock sinking deep into my flesh and I whimpered, trying to cope with the unexpected urge to suddenly offer him the gift of my virginity.

He didn't let me lose myself in my passionate wants for very long, because he shifted once more and climbed off the bed.

He started to get undressed.

A feeble-sounding mewl escaped my lips, unabated and unwanted. The corner of his lips turned up in a cocky grin. He'd heard me. Very slowly, he began to unbutton his shirt, revealing the dark blond nest of curls along his chest. The fabric opened up and the hard lines of his torso rippled in the shadows, catching my attention for far longer than I wanted them to.

My pussy tightened hard, and I couldn't help it.

He shrugged off that white button-up and tossed it on the chair by the window. Next, he kicked off his shoes and unbuttoned his slacks, pushing them down his hips. He stepped out of them and tossed them aside too. He sat down on the edge of the bed and pulled his socks off next.

He was wearing a dark, silky looking pair of boxers, but those didn't last much longer either. I couldn't take my eyes off of him as he pushed them down too. I lay there frozen, and he flew toward me, straddling my waist once more and pinning me to the bed.

Oh.

My.

Fuck.

His cock.

It was so hard and only inches from my face. I could see every thick ridge, every pulsing vein, and that all paled when I took in the sheer size of it. My pussy clenched down hard in anxious anticipation. Would it hurt if he fucked me? Would I like it? I didn't know.

I kind of... *wanted* to know though.

I hated myself for even thinking it. His body weight was heavy over mine and I knew that no matter how hard I bucked, there would be no escaping him.

He reached for me and pulled the sodden panties free from my lips.

"If you aren't going to talk, little human, I have a different use for that pretty mouth," he purred, and I hissed with fury. There could be no doubt of what he meant by that, not with his cock only inches from my lips.

The fucking audacity of this man.

"I'll bite clean through your cock if you try to put it in my mouth," I spat.

I wouldn't tell him that I sort of wanted to find out what he tasted like. I wouldn't tell him that I kind of needed to find out what his cock in my mouth would feel like.

"Good luck. Unless you have silver teeth, that won't do you much good," he chuckled, and I forced myself to look away from the throbbing monstrosity of a cock in front of my face.

My blood ran red hot.

He gripped my chin and turned my face right back with one hand before the other slapped my breast hard. His dark eyes held mine as they peppered my chest with hard spanks, catching the tips of my nipples over and over.

My cries echoed all around me, helpless and pitiful and weak. There was nothing to do but take it until he decided that he was through.

Casually, he transferred his weight backwards so that he could touch between my legs. I should have tried to close my thighs and keep him out, but I was ashamed to realize that I was instinctually opening for him, my hips rocking back and forth.

Was he going to fuck me now? Was I going to lose my virginity to a cruel monster?

Instead, he slid two fingers inside me, slowly. Surely. Arrogantly.

My pussy gripped them like a vise.

He pumped them in and out of me, teasing me and a wave of humiliation washed over me as my body reacted of its own accord, like a goddamn traitor. I was never going to get over how much I hated myself right now for responding that way.

His fingers fluttered inside me, and I moaned softly before he drew them out. Without even a second's hesitation, he forced them in between my lips.

"Suck. Taste yourself on my fingers and then tell me you don't want my cock in your mouth," he demanded.

Instinctually, I started to suck his fingers, tasting my own milky sweetness intermingled with the saltiness of his skin. He pushed them in and out of my mouth, going in deeper with every subsequent motion. I closed my eyes and the only thing on my mind was what his cock would taste like against my tongue.

I hated myself for thinking that. I hated myself for wanting that.

I cleaned his fingers off the best that I could. I could see something that was akin to pride in his gaze as I did what he commanded, and when he finally pulled his fingers from my mouth, I was hopeful that I had pleased him.

Without ceremony, he reached between my thighs and pinched my clit. Hard.

I keened, grappling with the painfully intense sensitivity of his punishing hand. I bucked as much as I was able, not an attempt to force him off of me, but more as a way to simply make it through the pain he was forcing on me. When he released my clit, I cried out with relief. He laid the pads of his fingers against my tender bundle of nerves, a silent warning that he wouldn't hesitate to chastise me that way again in a heartbeat.

I swallowed anxiously.

"I'm going to give you a choice. Either you're going to talk or you're going to suck my cock. Now choose. I can keep this up all night," he growled.

I knew one thing for certain. I knew that I couldn't keep up with him for that long. I had to choose one or the other, so I chose the lesser evil.

I opened my mouth.

His grin was victorious, and I suddenly grew very nervous about my choice.

His hand slid over top of the comforter on my bed until he cupped the back of my head. I would have thought it an act of tenderness until he slipped his cock between my lips.

He was so much bigger than I realized. My jaw seemed like it was too small for a man of his size and a sudden wave of fright poured over me, causing an icy chill to race down my spine.

I hadn't picked the lesser evil. I'd picked the greater one.

There was no period of acclimation. No slowly opening my throat. No exploration or mercy of any kind. None of that.

He started fucking my face and he fucked it hard.

There was nothing for me to do but take it.

"I'm going to teach you a lesson with my cock, bad girl. When I'm through with it, maybe then you'll know better than to refuse to answer my questions," he warned, and my eyes watered.

I tried to hold my mouth open, keep my teeth pulled back, but it was all in vain. Nothing I did granted me any sort of gentleness. My cheeks started to hurt first, and my lips soon followed. My mouth was too small to take him, so it wasn't long before the tip of his cock bumped against the ring of muscle at the back of my throat, and it hurt far more when he pushed past that. I gagged, but it didn't matter either. I tried to control my reflex to push him out, but it was difficult. I didn't know how.

It was a ruthless punishment. I knew that now.

I cried around his cock, shamefully gagged by his thick length. If I could have spoken, I would have begged for mercy. I would have said that I'd tell him whatever he wanted to know, but I couldn't. I wasn't going to be able to speak a word until he finished using my mouth as he saw fit.

As rough as he was, there was a sickening part of me that enjoyed being treated like this. My clit was pulsing hard as his cock throbbed against my tongue. My arousal was slick on my inner thighs, dripping down and I already knew there was a wet spot beneath me because I could feel its cool shameful touch against my skin.

Please.

I wanted him to fuck me. I wanted him to make me come again.

The fucking of my mouth went on and on and I couldn't stop the fresh wave of tears from streaming down my face from the sheer mercilessness of it.

It was at that point I gave in. My body took over and my mind fled.

I started to suckle him as enthusiastically as I could. I swirled my tongue around his length and as the shock of his roughness faded into helpless acceptance, I began to taste him.

He was salty, a touch sweet, and so entirely masculine. The taste of him only added to the vigorous possession of my mouth and I moaned around his length. With vigorous effort, I swallowed around him, again and again as his cock began to throb even harder against my tongue.

He roared and my pussy clenched tightly with anticipation.

"Only good girls get to swallow, don't they?" he growled.

I whined around his cock.

"You weren't a good girl, were you?" he continued dangerously.

He never stopped fucking my mouth.

Please.

Don't.

"Close your eyes," he demanded and without thinking I did.

I cried out. I wanted to be a good girl. I wanted to swallow for him. I wanted to beg him to let me show him that I could be good.

He didn't allow that.

Just when he was about to come, he pulled free from my lips and his thick seed coated my face. It spurted onto my forehead, my eyelids, and my cheeks. I hadn't had time to close my mouth, so some of it fell onto my tongue and my lips. It was all over my face and I whimpered.

He climbed off of me and grasped my left leg. I was so shell-shocked that I didn't notice that he bound my ankle with the remnants of my nightgown. By the time that I did, he'd already spread my legs wide open and was working on tying up the right.

His seed dripped down my face. More of it dripped onto my tongue.

He hadn't allowed me to swallow, but when I finally managed to close my mouth, I did just because it felt like I was defying him. The taste of his seed was bitter at first, but then a creamy salty sweetness followed and even though I felt humiliated by his rough use, I enjoyed that single moment of quiet rebellion.

Now fully bound, I was defenseless as he reached between my legs and pinched my clit firmly once more. I moaned, the sound so shamefully wanton that it made me blush.

"Please," I begged.

"You will lie here with my cum dripping down your face as punishment while I search your place for answers. Be a good girl. I think you understand now that I know how to deal with very bad ones," he murmured.

I did now. I really did.

He stood in front of the bed and stared between my thighs.

The effect of his gaze on me was staggering. I should be well past sated by now. I'd experienced pleasure at his hands that had physically shattered me, twice, but the look of his hungry eyes dancing over my soaked, sore flesh made me want more all over again. His stare darkened and I fidgeted just a little bit.

He said nothing, but the look in his eyes said everything.

He wasn't through with me. Not by a long shot.

"I will return for you, bad girl," he promised, and I watched with measured sadness as he walked out of the room.

My clit throbbed. If I wasn't bound, I would have made myself come with my own fingers. I wondered if he'd known that. I glanced down at my breasts, taking stock of my hard nipples and the bright pink marks his fingers had left behind on my pale skin.

For some reason, I found myself proud to wear them. The impressions from his teeth had long faded, but I swore I could still feel them and that made a jolt of arousal spark straight down to my clit.

My tongue poked out from between my lips, catching several drops of his seed. I cleaned off my lips as thoroughly as I could, feeling almost desperate to swallow every bit of it that I could.

With every swallow, I felt myself growing more defiant. I felt more like myself once again.

His cum began to grow cold on my face and I chewed my lower lip. My temporary rebellion faded, and I sniffled, suddenly overcome with emotion. I'm not certain how long he left me for, but by the time he walked back through the door the first wave of tears had begun to fall and was dripping down my face. I watched him come in and my body curled in a quiet sob as I tried to hide just how much his absence had affected me.

He sat down beside me, and he pressed a damp towel against my cheek. He began to wipe the cum and tears from my face and there was a certain tenderness in the way he did it that I didn't expect.

"There now, that's a good girl," he murmured.

He was so thorough and gentle as he cleaned my face and a single thread of guilt pulled at me for trying to defy him all this time. It took me a short while to realize that he'd taken the time to moisten the towel with warm water and that only made my guilt pang even harder. I looked down, unwilling to face the fact that I'd thought him kind, not even for a moment.

"You took my cock so very well, little human. Such a very good girl," he whispered, and my heart swelled with pride for some unknown reason.

"You came back," I answered. I wasn't certain if I believed he was sitting here beside me or if this had all been nothing but a dream. I felt somewhere in the middle of reality and fantasy, as if my brain was captured in a hazy fog.

"I did. I'm a man of my word," he replied, and I believed him.

He was quiet for a while, inspecting my face for something. I wasn't sure what.

"I still have questions that need answers, but we need to deal with something first, don't we?" he asked, and my stomach dropped precipitously with both nerves and sudden unfathomable arousal. His fingers dropped to cup my pussy, gliding along the incredible wetness that had seemingly developed in his absence.

"You're soaking wet, so much wetter than when I left you," he observed softly.

A quiet squeak echoed all around me.

"I'm going to need to take care of this," he murmured, and I was ashamed to realize that my hips were rocking against his touch.

This had all gone to my head and there was nothing I could do to bring it back.

The surface of his fingers pressed firmly against my aching clit. I pressed back against him.

"I'm going to fuck this soaking wet little pussy until you're sore enough that you'll feel it all day tomorrow. That is already decided. The only part of this that is up to you now is whether I fuck your naughty little bottom afterwards and that depends on whether or not you tell me what I want to know."

For a split second, I considered telling him about my father's murder, how my family had been ruined by his villainous conduct and that the Venuti were probably at fault for some sort of deal gone wrong, but I stopped. I remembered myself and I blinked back tears. There was a part of me that wanted to tell him, but he was a monster too. He was a criminal, and all of this was probably just some terrible form of torture designed to give him the answers he wanted before he killed me. I couldn't trust him. Not now. Not ever.

Knowing I had no other choice, I just shook my head.

I refused him. Again.

"You should know that the scent of your arousal is only increasing, little human. You continue to fight me, but you can't stop thinking about what it's going to feel like when my cock takes your tight little pussy for the very first time," he observed.

I gritted my teeth.

"Tell me something, little human. Has anyone else ever touched that pretty bottom hole before?" he pressed. I drew in a shocked breath, unable to hide the surprise that surged through me instantly.

Instinctively, I pressed my thighs together. I didn't want to know where this was going next.

"No," I sputtered.

"Have you touched that tight little hole?" he pressed, and I couldn't stop the way my breath pulled in noisily all around me.

He couldn't know. There was no way.

My face flushed hard, and my legs spread for him. It was an unconscious reaction and entirely involuntary, and I couldn't stop it. My body had long since taken over the sound logic of my mind. By the ravenous look on his face that followed, he'd seen it too.

I had touched myself back there. One time and I'd never told anyone about it.

What happens in Vegas, stays in Vegas. Right?

It was after my friend's bachelorette party, and I'd been pretty drunk. She'd given out gift bags and I'd only opened it after I'd staggered back into the safety of my hotel room to find a small steel butt plug and a packet of lubricant. I'd only used a little bit of the lube before I'd rather hastily pushed the plug inside me. The rubber band of pain after I'd pushed it all the way inside was far more sobering than I ever wanted to admit. The strange part of the whole thing that once the ache had faded to something of a gradual smolder, I'd left it inside me because I'd found myself so turned on that I'd needed to come right after I'd put it in.

Worse than that, I'd used my vibrator on my clit because I'd needed to and before him, it had been the hardest orgasm I'd ever had in my life.

I didn't tell my friend. I didn't tell anyone. It was my secret to keep, and I wasn't about to give it up to the likes of a wolf.

I refused to answer him.

His eyes narrowed with dark promise.

He tore through the binds that held my ankles like they were made of tissue.

"What are you doing?" I shrieked.

"Only human men fuck their women on their back," he replied. "I'm not human and I'm not going to fuck you that way."

Roughly, he flipped me over on my stomach and I yelped when he placed one hand in the middle of my back and the other on top of my bare bottom.

I'm not sure why, but him looking at my naked backside was the most embarrassing part of this whole ordeal. I could feel myself blushing hard and his palm smoothed over the surface of my skin. He cupped each cheek, and I was left with the harrowing thought of how his hand dwarfed each side of my ass. His hands were so very big. I found myself pressing back into the hard plane of his palm and just when I thought maybe he was being gentle before he fucked me, he spanked me hard.

I whimpered out loud and a second cruel smack followed.

I was getting the first real spanking of my life. I soon lost count of how many times his palm connected with my bare cheeks. His smacks were relentless and quick and far harder than I was ready for.

I was in so far over my head.

"Stop! You have no right to spank me!" I shrieked.

It hurt so much that I was beginning to fear that I was losing grip of the very last semblances of my control, of my sanity, of everything that made me who I am.

"I do, pretty human. I want this little bottom bright red before I force every last inch of my cock into that tight virgin pussy," he smirked with amusement.

"Please!"

"It makes me very hard when you beg for mercy, sweet girl, but it's not going to rescue you from the thorough spanking you've had coming since you first refused me," he countered.

I cried out, feeling helpless.

With his hand in the center of my back, I couldn't roll to the side. I couldn't avoid even a single one. His hand was relentless and the longer my spanking continued, the more I convinced myself that his palm must be made of wood. He punished the upper curves of my cheeks, all the way down to the middle of my thighs.

I was his prisoner. His to do with as he wished. His to hurt. His to fuck.

"Please stop," I pleaded. My voice broke and he started spanking the backs of my thighs exclusively. "Please, alpha. Please," I begged. Over and over, I tried to appeal to his sympathy. There had been a glimmer of it when he'd cleaned off my face, but it was nowhere to be seen now.

He intended to punish me, and he wanted it to hurt.

It did. So much.

My mind edged at a dark place, teetering on that thin border and I squeezed my eyes shut, just trying to survive before I fell apart.

My entire focus was centered on his hand spanking my backside. It was as if he was branding me with fire with every strike and it was only that much more intense when he punished the backs of my thighs. My hips arched back and forth, and my cries grew louder. Was he going to make me cry? Was that what he wanted? I was terrified that I would.

Would my tears be enough to set me free?

"Your spanking will end when you lift that pretty bottom for me. Present me with that soaking wet little pussy so that I can fuck it," he demanded.

I didn't even think.

I just obeyed.

I arched my back and spread my legs, only to earn a very quick flurry of spanks on the sensitive flesh of my inner thighs.

My mouth opened in shock, desperate for air and his punishing smacks stopped.

"Good girl," he murmured.

My heartbeat nearly skipped a beat at the words of praise.

My bottom burned hot, but my pussy burned far hotter. The hard punishment, the rough humiliating treatment was turning me into a soaking wet mess of arousal and need and red-hot desire. He grabbed my hips and lifted me up onto my knees. With my wrists still bound, I couldn't reach back or do anything to fight him off.

Not that I wanted to.

I should want to.

But I didn't.

My pussy ached. It felt so empty, and I knew now that it would soon be very full of this cruel bastard's deliciously massive cock.

And I couldn't wait.

"You were wet when I left you covered with my seed, and even wetter when I returned after leaving you to wonder about what might happen next, but you're absolutely soaked now that you've been very thoroughly spanked," he observed.

I shivered with shame. I'd lost my grip on reality.

I was a prisoner to his wants, his needs, and the worst part of it all was that they had become mine too.

"Do you know what else I can see, little human?"

"No," I whispered hoarsely.

"I can see your tight little bottom hole practically quivering in anticipation of being fucked there too," he added, and I squeaked with embarrassment knowing that he could see such a shameful thing and that only made it tighten even more in absolute terror and unfathomable arousal.

The next thing I knew the head of his cock was poised against my entrance. It was scalding hot, and I forgot how to breathe. And then it was inside me.

All of it. In a single brutal thrust.

He breached my virginity without warning and without apology. My entire core blazed hot with fire. My arousal eased his entry, but it still hurt so much more than I imagined it would. He was so big, and my body felt too small and too tight around him. His girth stretched my pussy so widely that even though I was crying out for him to get out, he refused. Instead, he pushed so deeply inside me that his pelvis pressed against the scalded cheeks of my backside.

My pussy clutched hard at him, convulsing with pain and extremely reluctant pleasure as I tried to get used to the sheer size of him inside me.

And then he began to move, and my fucking truly began.

I closed my eyes, trying to grapple with the demons inside me and utterly failing.

I was a prisoner beneath him, held captive by his cock. I knew that I wouldn't be set free until I broke all over his cock.

There was not even an ounce of tenderness in the way he took me. He used my pussy brutally hard and viciously fast, mounting me like the savage beast I knew he was. My pussy burned from the start, and I knew that his promise to ensure that I felt him tomorrow would be kept.

When this was over, I was going to be very sore. Panic fell over me in waves. I grappled with fear and longing. I warred with my pride. I shouldn't want to be treated like this.

It shouldn't be making me *wetter*.

It shouldn't make me want to orgasm. *Again.*

My pussy was so wet that I could hear it with every single thrust of his hard cock. I would have been embarrassed, but his practically feral use of my body held my entire focus.

It hurt so very much at first, but once I reached a certain point, I fell off the edge of something else. My desire hurtled through me with wild abandon, rising higher and higher despite everything in my head that demanded I fight it. My pleasure held me captive, and I feared when it finally reigned free, it would destroy me.

He leaned over me and gripped my shoulder with one hand, using my own body as leverage to fuck me even harder than before. With his other hand, he reached around and captured my clit between his fingers.

My arousal escalated tenfold.

With far too knowledgeable fingers, he stoked my need until I was practically shivering with it in his arms. His cock continued to pound into me brutally hard, a daunting reminder of his strength and power over me, but his touch played across my clit like a lover's caress. He varied the pressure of his fingertips, slowly building me up so that he could tear me apart.

It wouldn't take very long.

Even with the aching pain of the hard fucking he was forcing me to take, my pleasure soon raged forth like a hurricane. In seconds, I was overwhelmed and consumed by the incredible sensations warring inside my innocent body. My core twisted hard, and I knew I was tiptoeing along the edge of exquisite ecstasy and cruel agony. As his fingers worked my clit and his cock thrust into me ruthlessly hard, I remained uncertain which sensation would win out.

But I didn't have a choice. I was going to take one or the other whether I liked it or not. I trembled and shook beneath him and then something inside me snapped.

I screamed his name.

I lost my grip on reality, bridging into the dark world of savage pleasure and ruthless insanity.

My release shattered me into a million different pieces, like shards of glass that would never be put back together again. My legs shook and the physical devastation that followed was so incredibly powerful that I wondered if I could ever go back to being myself after it was all over. My toes curled and my nails dug into the pads of my hands as I suffered on that thin edge of pain and pleasure far more powerful than I'd ever known.

My orgasm went on and on and on.

My mouth opened in a circle, and I gasped, desperate for air and finding none.

I couldn't tell up from down or left from right. All I knew was that my pussy gripped his cock so hard that I feared it might force him out, but it didn't. My nipples peaked against the surface of my bed, still sore and aching from the punishing pinches and bites he'd put them through. The more I arched into him, the more they scraped into the comforter and the more I realized that I was doing it on purpose.

I wanted it to hurt.

I was coming this hard because it did.

I screamed for him and by the time the orgasm finally began to fade away into the edges of pure bliss, my voice was hoarse, and a wave of exhaustion surged through me.

But he didn't stop.

I whimpered fearfully. He didn't show a single sign that he was starting to slow down.

My satisfied need withered away, only to be replaced with a growing anxiety that I wasn't going to make it through this. As if he could read my thoughts, his fingers returned to pet my clit and I tried to jerk away from him as an electric surge of discomfort raced through me at his touch.

"I can't. Please," I cried out with panic. I wanted to push his hands away, but I couldn't break my own free.

"You can and you will. You're going to come again for me and I'm going to mark this pretty little pussy with my seed, little mate," he murmured.

Mate.

He'd called me his mate.

There was no more time to think. My fucking began again, and I descended back into that dark painful place once more. My ability to focus on anything but the thick cock surging between my thighs fled.

His rough touch pressed against the overly sensitive bundle of nerves even harder, making me scream, and I didn't stop. I begged for mercy. I pleaded for forgiveness. I told him I'd do anything if he'd stop forcing me to come for him. His fingers mercilessly worked my clit, driving me into the world of pleasure and barely manageable pain once more. Real fear mixed in with the ecstasy and agony and I found myself wondering if I could even survive through yet another orgasm.

I cried out, drowning within the varying emotions that flew through me at his dominant hand. His cock never stopped slamming into me, possessing me, and reminding me that in our world, I was the human and he was the monster.

He was teaching me that my proper place was beneath him and that was the most powerful feeling of all.

I tried to rush back to the surface and reclaim what I'd lost, but I'd long passed the point of having control. I'd lost it somewhere in my own bed. Maybe I'd never even had it in the first place. Maybe he'd taken it the moment he'd first set his eyes on me.

Against my will, I could feel myself approaching a fourth orgasm. I could tell that it was going to be brutally hard and that more than anything, it was going to hurt considerably.

I panicked, but it didn't matter. He pushed on anyway.

As much as I tried to fight it, he forced it forward, and it poured over me like a pot of boiling water.

From deep within, a blazing fire surged forth, hurtling through my veins and scorching through every last inch of me. I began to scream, just trying to survive the overwhelming storm of pleasure and intensely hot agony that scalded me from within. My core twisted hard, and my clit pulsed with one jolt of aching sensation over and over again until I lost every bit of myself.

I thrashed beneath him. I writhed into his thrusts, taking him deeper and deeper until I felt his massive girth throb inside me. He roared with his own pleasure, and it forced my orgasm even higher, throwing me into a pleasurable panic as I suffered for him while wholly impaled on his cock.

His seed spurted deep inside me, fiery whiplashes of cum that lashed inside me so hot that I feared that it might brand my pussy with his mark. He pounded into me, enjoying every last second of his orgasm as he conquered me with every inch of his big cock.

That final release broke me, and I soared into the heavens.

I floated somewhere in a dark void in the seconds following that orgasm. It was free of the worries of the world and everything that troubled and scared me. It was a beautiful place, so very peaceful and so wonderful that I found myself wanting to stay there forever.

It was the blissful numbness of complete and utter surrender.

His soft touch brought my head very slowly back to Earth. His touch was tender and soft, and it took me several minutes to realize he'd freed my hands. Carefully, he began to massage my shoulders, probably to help soothe tension, but I was so well satisfied and dazed that I felt nothing of the sort. He gathered me in his arms and arranged me so that I was on my side facing his chest. He wound his arms around my waist and pulled me firmly against him.

I blinked several times and I realized that my cheeks were wet. When I licked my lips, they tasted salty, and it eventually dawned on me that final orgasm had been so powerful that I'd started to cry. My sobs quickened and my body racked forward and in some crazy place in the insanity of it all, I clutched at him with my fingers as though he could save me from myself.

There wasn't any strength left in my body. My legs felt like jelly. Even the prospect of pushing myself up to a seated position in my own bed seemed like too daunting a task.

"Shhh, my sweet mate. I think that's enough for you today," he said gently, his breath tickling the tiny hairs along my earlobe. I cried harder for a time until I could pull myself together enough to quiet my sobs and slow my tears.

Timidly, I curled into him, pressing my forehead against his chest at first before I turned my head and laid my cheek against it. The pounding of his heartbeat was loud, but soothing and for several long minutes I just listened to it. My breathing started to normalize, and I shivered as the heat began to bleed out of me at an alarming rate. My body temperature was dropping and fast. I started to tremble so hard that my teeth chattered.

He moved so quickly that I couldn't keep up with him, but he lifted me cleanly off the bed and tucked me under the covers. He dove underneath the sheets with me and pulled me back to him, offering me his body heat along with it.

As the minutes passed, I started to feel more like myself. I could feel the sweat evaporating off my skin and his thick milky seed dripping down my thighs. If I had more energy, I would have gotten up to clean myself up, but I was so exhausted that I didn't really care about how filthy I felt with it drying on my legs.

In fact, I kind of liked it.

The more the numbing bliss faded away, the more I began to feel the aching soreness throughout my limbs and even more so between my thighs. Not too long after that, I finally braved a chance and looked up at him through damp tear-soaked lashes.

"You're so beautiful like this, little mate," he murmured, and his compliment made me blush unexpectedly. I bashfully bit my bottom lip, not knowing what to say so I didn't say anything at all.

"You should know I'm not through with you yet, not by a long shot," he added, and a soft sound of desperation fled my lips.

"Your refusal to answer my questions still needs to be dealt with, but I'll save your bottom fucking for another time when you're not so worn out and I can really enjoy taking that tight little hole," he whispered, and I shivered at the same time that his hand slid down the arch of my spine. I whimpered softly when he continued his exploration until he slid a finger down the cleft of my backside.

He slid far enough to cup my pussy first. Then, he gathered the wetness that was still seeping from me with his finger, and he returned to find my bottom hole, vulnerable and unprotected and he took advantage of that.

"Don't! Please!" I yelped, my voice still incredible shaky from what he'd already put me through.

"You've got so much more coming, little mate. I'm going to give you just a taste," he purred.

Without thinking, I tensed hard, and he roughly forced a single thick finger inside my bottom hole. I tried to clench my cheeks to keep him out, but he was too strong. He growled as my tight ring of muscle tightened immeasurably hard around him, unused to taking anyone or anything back there for a very long time.

Pain blazed up and down my spine for several long moments and the tears that had fallen already threatened to return once more.

"Please," I begged. "Please take it out."

"I'll be back for you tomorrow, sweet mate, and by the time I'm finished with you, you're going to ask me to fuck you here. You're going to beg me to make it hurt," he purred.

"I won't," I vowed, and he smiled with amusement.

I swallowed hard. He'd already proven himself to be a man of his word.

I hid my face in the crook of his shoulder, feeling my body tremble against him as he roughly pumped his finger in and out of my bottom. The feeling of that thick digit was painful and entirely too foreign, and I hated how it made my sore pussy tighten with anticipation.

Good girls weren't supposed to getting their bottom holes fingered. Good girls especially didn't think about getting their asses fucked.

But I was.

And it was making my clit zing with unwelcome desire. Maybe I was a bad girl.

Maybe I was his bad girl.

Whatever. I didn't want to think about it anymore.

I did know that I wouldn't be anywhere near here tomorrow night. I wasn't going to lie here and wait for him to arrive and fuck my bottom hole with his ginormous cock.

That was a worry for tomorrow though. I was too tired to think about it anymore today. I closed my eyes and fell asleep, still safely encased in his arms and surrounded by the security of his scent.

And to be honest…

I liked it.

CHAPTER 4

Lawson
The next day...

I couldn't get her off my mind. No one had ever stood up to me like her before. Her constant defiance made me curious, and I hadn't stopped thinking about her since I'd left her safe and sound and sleeping in her bed that morning.

I'd used every resource at my disposal to learn more about her. I scanned over every public record available from her birth certificate to her credit report and to her rather impressive grades at the ritzy private college she'd attended. She was highly intelligent, daughter to a famous professor of mechanical engineering, at least until he'd lost it and shot up the French Quarter last year.

I remembered that day like it was yesterday. The city had gone wild with fear until he'd been put down by a group of men brave enough to stand up against him.

I'd thought nothing of it. It had been simply a human matter that had gotten out of hand. One that had nothing to do with me, my pack, or the vampires that dared to walk my streets.

Looking at it now though, I wasn't convinced that I'd been right.

I couldn't shake the feeling that maybe I'd overlooked something that day, that maybe it wasn't just the simple massacre that I'd thought it to be. Curious now, I pulled open every news article that I could find. I read about her father's history, the psychologist's diagnosis, and finally, I clicked through to a news article that focused on the men who had stopped the whole thing from becoming worse than it already was.

I scrolled down to a picture of the group of five men. I paused and at first, I was unsure why, but then I studied the men even more closely.

I enlarged the picture, narrowing in on one man in particular. There was something about him that looked familiar, and I couldn't quite place it.

He was wearing contacts, dark ones. I could see the outline of them around his irises. I sat back and imagined him with red eyes, and it finally clicked.

He was the lead security guard that had charged into the Venuti prison. He was a vampire.

I'd bet good money that the rest of the men with him were vampires too. When I zoomed in on the other men, I realized they were all wearing contacts, all of them wearing a dark enough color to hide the bright red that gave away their true identities.

Last night, the mistrust in Ava's eyes had been blatant and perhaps this was a part of the reason for that. She wouldn't have talked no matter what I'd done to her last night, but that didn't mean I was giving up on her. There were other ways I could break her, and I would keep trying until she gave me exactly what I wanted. I wanted to learn everything about her, and I wouldn't give up until I did.

I wouldn't give up until I made her mine completely.

Last night, I'd had the forethought to slip a tiny tracking device inside her without her knowing. I'd done it when I'd forced my finger into her virgin little bottom. I moved my mouse and opened the tracking software, and I swore out loud as soon as the indicator flared to life on my screen.

I'd known she probably wouldn't be in her own bed when I came for her tonight, but I certainly hadn't expected her to be back inside the Venuti tower either.

Crafty girl. Fucking reckless too.

The little spitfire of a human had somehow made it back into the hornets' nest of vampires and I didn't know how she'd managed it. To be honest, it was so impressive that it was making my cock very, very hard as I thought about what I would to do her to make her tell me why she was so dead set on putting herself in one deadly situation after the next.

Hard enough to give her the hard bottom fucking she not only needed, but sorely deserved.

I'd been preparing myself for another fight when I went to her tonight. I had expected her to hide out somewhere to avoid what she had coming, but I wasn't prepared for this. I'd had my men watching her home since I'd left in the early morning hours, and she'd somehow given them the slip. I hadn't wanted to leave her without protection. I feared for her safety, especially when she had access to knowledge that would undoubtedly get her killed by any number of vampires or shifters should anyone else find out about it.

Before I'd left, I'd watched her sleep for hours, enamored by the angelically peaceful look on her face. Her cheeks never lost the beautifully pink hue from the orgasms I'd forced on her. Her body shivered for quite a bit of time after she fell asleep, her breathing even and soft and truly musical to hear. I'd kept her warm with my elevated body temperature and when I was finally convinced that she was in a deep enough slumber for me to leave, I'd slipped out of her bedroom without a sound.

She hadn't even stirred.

The vampire clan hadn't come for her there. I was sure of it. My men would have seen something if they tried. Instead, she probably snuck by my men somehow and made it back into the vampire fortress all on her own.

The part I was terribly unsure of was whether she went there willingly or not.

I chewed my lip and tried to figure out what to do next. I didn't know whether I wanted to fuck her or spank her. Probably both.

I rolled my upper lip and stroked my hand up and down my cock, remembering the delicious moan that I had elicited from her when I'd punished her naughty little bottom hole with just my middle finger.

Her bottom had been so tight around it. I had no doubt that it would feel that much tighter when I punished it with my cock. I couldn't wait to hear her cries and whimpers, her fear and desire for me to fuck her there harder. I was going to enjoy every last moment when I finally took that virgin hole. I would take it all.

I'd known the moment that I'd thrust my cock into her delicious virgin pussy that she was mine. She wasn't just a woman to me now. She was my mate whether she wanted to be or not. There would be no choice in the matter for her.

I was going to possess her.

Own her in every physical sense of the word.

I was going to be her life, her everything.

I didn't care if she didn't want it at first. It was simply a matter of time until she begged for it, until I decided it was time to mark her as mine.

She was my destiny. I could feel it deep in the marrow of my bones.

My cock was so hard it felt like an iron spike. I closed my eyes, remembering the way her beautiful body writhed beneath mine with pleasure. Her skin had glowed with the most gorgeous sheen of perspiration, clear evidence of her loss of control at my hands.

I growled, feeling my arousal settle at the base of my spine. My thumb grazed up and down the fabric of my slacks as I thought about the little minx before I finally managed to pull my hand away.

I'd never lost control like this. Not for anyone.

Ever.

It was deeply unnerving, and I didn't know how to handle it, but I knew that it wasn't time to give into my desire no matter how much I wanted it.

There would be time for it later when she was back in my arms and then I would show her that there was a much better place for me to mark with my seed that wasn't in the palm of my own hand.

The next time I came it would be with my cock deep in my mate's disobedient little bottom because I'd made a promise and I intended to keep it.

With a sigh, I turned my gaze back to the map on my screen. It still showed Ava to be somewhere within the Venuti tower and I would bet money on the fact that she wasn't a guest in one of their hotel rooms. It was possible she could once again be trapped in a prison cell or sneaking through the building on a mission seeking out God knows what. Either way, I'd bet money on the fact that it wasn't for anything good.

I scratched my chin thoughtfully.

I was going to go after her. I'd lost too many members of my pack the last time, however. This was something I was going to have to do on my own. I wasn't willing to risk their lives when I was off chasing my mate.

I picked up my cell phone and called my second in command. In some mafia circles, he'd be known as a consigliore, but in my world, he was my beta and that meant so much more than a basic mobster definition. He picked up on the first ring just like I knew he would.

"What's up, boss? You're agitated. I can feel it," Toboe said knowingly. The bond between an alpha and beta was stronger than the rest of the members of my pack. This wasn't the first time he'd sensed my inner turmoil and I knew it wouldn't be the last.

"Come up to my office. I need to talk to you," I answered impatiently.

"On my way," he replied, and I hung up the phone. I pushed myself up from my desk and wandered over to the window that overlooked my property, watching the guards patrol the perimeter fence with a rising sense of irritation.

This was my sanctuary outside the quarter, the place we could oversee the city that my ancestors and now I had reigned over with an iron fist for centuries. Even though it was early evening, and the sun was just beginning to dip on the horizon, I could see the flashing lights of Canal Street. The quarter never really slept and if anything, it was just beginning to wake up for what would most certainly be a long night for tourists and locals alike.

I ruled over most of the territory of New Orleans from here. We'd operated the ports here for the majority of the city's history, controlling what came into the city and what was sent out, which ultimately meant we governed the financial well-being of New Orleans.

Sometimes that meant getting your hands dirty. Sometimes that involved the drug trade, or the smuggling of shifters or humans in and out of the city, but ultimately, we were an organization that was based in money, power, and influence. In concept, my pack operated similarly to the Italian mafia families, but we were far more influential and far more well connected than that. We'd been established here for a long time and that afforded us the kind of wealth and power that people could only dream of. We'd helped build this city from the ground up, but it didn't stop there.

There was a member of my pack at every level of human government here in the city and within the state of Louisiana. There wasn't a single law or ordinance passed without my explicit approval and if anyone ever thought to stand against me, they were quickly dealt with in a way that made sure they thought of nothing but obedience or else they were silenced forever, only to be replaced with someone who would be loyal to me and me alone.

I had my hands in every bank, every business no matter how small. Nothing happened in my city without me knowing about it, except in the case of Venuti territory. They furrowed their way into my city, using their own power and wealth to make a stronghold of their own despite years of fighting against them.

The Venuti Clan had long since been my enemy, but we'd come to a peace agreement about fifteen years ago that held on by a tenuous thread at best. I was constantly putting out fires in an effort to keep them and my pack from an all-out war, and that was a full-time job all by itself. Honestly, the Venuti were a thorn in my side that I'd be grateful to rid myself of, but I wouldn't risk my pack to do it. That is, unless I could get my hands on the bullets that Ava had. That could be enough to changes the tides of war between my pack and the Venuti.

It might be enough to push the Venuti out of my city once and for all.

The door to my office opened and closed behind me and I turned back from my view of the city to see that Toboe had entered the room.

He sat down in the chair in front of my desk and cocked his head to the side. Casually, he sniffed the air and the tiniest smirk edged at the corner of his mouth.

"Don't you dare," I warned.

"You positively reek of human female," he observed carefully, his eyes dancing with amusement. I rolled my lip in kind.

"What of it?" I snarled, daring him to challenge me.

"I recognize her scent," he continued as he crossed his arms over his chest. His shoulders rounded. He wouldn't stand up against me. He knew better than that.

I took a deep breath and reminded myself of his loyalty so that I didn't tear his head off.

"I need to go back into the Venuti tower," I said, attempting to change the subject even though I knew it probably wouldn't work.

"Is that where she is?" he pressed, and I snarled openly in aggravation.

"She knows something, and I need to get it out of her," I replied curtly.

"You need to fuck it out of her is what you mean," he chuckled.

I glared at him with frustration. I didn't need to answer for him to recognize that he was right.

"Did she tell you where she got those bullets from when you went to question her last night?" he asked, and I shook my head. He clicked his tongue in mock disapproval and shook his head. "Losing your touch then, boss..." he observed lightly, and I growled in warning before he put his hands up in defense. By the look on his face, he was blatantly ignoring my annoyance in his volley for more information.

Typically, I allowed him to speak freely, but with my mate somewhere within the clutches of my enemy, I felt far more agitated than usual. I was on edge; any sudden thing could set me off and I only barely recognized that it was her. My mate was in danger, and it was making me see red. I wouldn't rest until she was safe in my arms, no matter if she came willingly or her bottom was marked with my belt.

He must have sensed my worry because his face softened, and he nodded once. He didn't need to say it, but he quickly recognized how serious this was to me.

"Tell me what you did find out, boss," he said, his tone softer this time. I sighed and I began to explain myself. "Tell me how I can help."

"I've never seen anything like her. You know how rare it is for humans to know of the existence our kind. It's even rarer for her to know how to kill us. She sleeps with a wooden stake and a silver knife by her bed, for God's sake. She knows far more than any normal human should," I started.

"It's also pretty abnormal that she has a gun that makes such an incredible display of the unlucky vampire set in her sights. Like a fucking firework show," he said bluntly, eliciting a chuckle from me. "Boom," he added while spreading his fingers wide, mimicking the brilliant spectacle.

Even in some of my surliest moods, he could always get me to laugh. Some of the other alpha kingpins I'd been in contact with over the years that reigned elsewhere refused to tolerate such behavior, citing disrespect as the root cause. My father had been one of those, but I found Toboe's humor endearing. I believed that kinship and loyalty bred a much more powerful pack rather than one ruled by fear, and thus far I'd managed to grow our reach that much farther using that strategy. As far as I was concerned, I'd been successful.

"I don't know how she did it, but she managed to slip by Genzo and some of the other wolves keeping watch over her house. I'd known she was pretty crafty from how she was in the Venuti tower last week, and just how defiant she was with me last night, so I slipped a tracker inside her so that I could monitor her movements. Somehow, she's back in the Venuti tower with the vampires again. I can't track her exact location in the building until I'm inside it, so I'm going to have to go in and retrieve her myself," I explained, and his mouth set in a grim line. His expression turned serious, and I already knew what he was going to say before he said it.

"No," I growled.

"You know I'm coming with you," he said.

"I can't have you with me. It's far too dangerous," I started to clarify, and he shook his head.

"Don't you dare try to keep me from coming with you," he countered, and I sat back with a sigh. He knew I could make him stay if I wanted to. If I commanded him using the power of my alpha, he'd be forced to obey me. I'd never had to do that with Toboe before and I was extremely reluctant to begin now.

"Don't. I'm asking you not to," he added.

I gritted my teeth and he pushed further.

"You need someone to watch your back, alpha. Let me do my job as your beta," he demanded.

"Dammit, Toboe," I muttered. "I'm not going to convince you to just let me go in alone, am I?"

He grinned widely and shook his head. I sighed, knowing I wasn't going to win this argument without force. If he wanted to risk his skin in order to protect me, I would allow him.

"Listen. I just want to kill as many of those pointy toothed fuckers as I can, especially after they reneged on the deal that *they* made last time and took me prisoner," he said rather angrily.

"They really need to get their newbie vamp population under control. There can only be so many deaths attributed to the drunk and disorderly in this city. Hell, there were so many of them that I had to have the investigators start blaming them on alligators. Fucking ridiculous," I mused.

A very long time ago, there was a peace agreement made in order to stop the bloodshed from the constant fighting between shifters and vampires. Humans were not to know of the existence of our species and right now, the Venuti were doing a shit job of keeping up with their part. They wanted more than they already had. They thought they deserved even more. Power. Money. God knows what.

If my suspicions were correct, they wanted to rule over more than just the quarter. They probably wanted to conquer the human world after that too.

I couldn't be certain, not just yet. If the evidence presented itself, I would be forced to take measures that would involve more than just our two families. I'd have to call in the reigning families all across North America. If it was a big enough problem, that could involve those all around the world.

This could be really big and really dangerous. I just needed to know more before I did anything drastic.

The signs were there though. I was sure of it.

For years I'd been trying to work with the Venuti to get them to follow a set of more ironclad rules so that we could keep our existence secret from humankind, but they spat on those efforts at every turn. They felt the need to constantly sire new vampires. I didn't know if they were trying to build an army or what, but I did know that they couldn't control them enough to keep them hunting in their own territories. More often than not, they crossed the boundaries and fed in the districts in which I reigned. It had been a source of conflict between our families for a very long time.

This last time I'd gone far enough to send Toboe in my stead, but they'd taken him hostage in an attempt to get to me instead. I'd lost valuable men getting him back.

Ava Winters was priceless though. If I was able to get my hands on those exploding light bullets, it could turn the tides of power here in New Orleans. It could be enough for me to push the Venuti out of the city once and for all, which was a very tempting thought. All that considered, however, I was still going to fuck that pretty little bottom when I finally got my hands on her.

That just made me want to find her even more.

"So, what's the plan, boss?" Toboe finally asked. I took a deep breath and started to lay it all out.

"You will meet with Genzo. Get him to supply us with some stealthy tech that will get us through the Venuti tower as quietly as we can. After last time, I won't allow anyone other than you to come with me. Make that crystal fucking clear to the rest of the pack, you get me?"

"Fully fucking transparent, boss," he replied.

"I'm serious. You and no one else."

"You can count on me, boss," he added and this time his tone was somber. I knew he would obey me on this, and I cleared my throat thoughtfully, trying to think of what else we might need.

"I also want some guns with wooden bullets at the very least. If the vamps are gonna shoot at us with silver bullets, we're going to shoot right back at them," I added. It wouldn't be an exploding bullet of light, but it would be more than enough as long as we shot them in the heart.

"Definitely. They won't know what hit them," he answered.

"Oh, and Toboe?"

"Yeah?"

"When we're through dealing with the Venuti, you're going to assist in teaching my mate a lesson she won't ever forget," I snarled.

"Your mate, huh?" he asked.

I nodded once, my gaze hard and unforgiving.

"Once we get her back here safe and sound, I'm going to take her upstairs and make her truly mine. By tomorrow morning, she will bear my mark and tomorrow, I'm going to introduce her to the pack," I said firmly.

He grinned widely.

"You got it, boss," he responded, and I knew he meant every word.

* * *

In less than an hour, the two of us were on our way to the tower. I had my driver take us to the entryway of the tunnel we'd broken into just a few days ago and I was surprised to find it mostly intact. There were a few caved-in areas and several more that were slightly flooded even though it hadn't rained all week, but we were able to easily jump over those and make our way through without much trouble. Once we reached the blast area, we found that the Venuti had only just begun repairs.

Arrogant motherfuckers. I'd have dealt with this weak point days ago.

Maybe they didn't expect to get invaded by wolves twice in one week. If it had been my turf, repairs and reinforcement would have been started the very next day. I would have had countless men stationed to guard it and protect it from attack.

Unexpectedly, there wasn't a single guard inside the prison. There were a number of captives still safely contained within the cells, but I made no move to break them out whether they were shifter or vampire. I'd gotten Toboe out several days ago. No one else from my pack was down here so I wasn't going to waste any time, especially with my mate still in danger.

Oddly enough, Ava wasn't any of them either, but I was more than certain she'd been here at some point because there were at least half a dozen Venuti security guards lying headless on the floor, likely the result of her special anti-vamp light bullets.

Honestly, it was pretty impressive and quite arousing to behold.

Ava Winters was a little badass, but more important, she was my little badass. In a weird way, I was proud of her for it. I wasn't used to feeling anything like it, so I tried to push it aside and just focus on finding her.

I keyed into the software on my phone, trying to pinpoint her location. The app indicated that she was several floors above us and when I turned to tell Toboe, he pointed down the hallway where there was another vampire lying dead.

"I bet if we follow her trail of deliciously bloody breadcrumbs, we'll find her," he said softly, and I snorted with quiet laughter.

"You know, that's not a half bad idea," I muttered.

"I know. I'm a goddamn genius. I deserve a raise," he replied lightly.

I raised my eyebrow and stared right at him.

"It was worth a shot," he muttered, and I shook my head, more than a little amused.

"It was a valid effort," I snorted.

"So, you'll think about it?" he asked hopefully.

"Definitely not," I answered.

"I'm so undervalued and underpaid around here," he complained, but I could tell he was smirking just from the way he said it.

"I know. I don't even know why you're still here," I countered.

"I stick around in hopes that one day you'll appreciate me. With a big fat paycheck," he mused.

"I wouldn't count on it," I said with a wink.

He pouted in mock disappointment, but his expression turned serious as the two of us studied the mangled body she'd left behind. It was something of a bloody mess. No matter how many times I saw it, the gory scene her little weapon left behind was jarring.

"Come on. Let's find my pretty little vampire slayer. I want answers and she's going to give them to me," I snarled. I took off down the hall, following the path of dead vamps around the corner into an open staircase.

"Damn right," Toboe grinned, and I heard him take off after me.

"Guess she went up from here," I observed, taking in another grisly sight of the mutilated remains of another headless torso. I took a deep breath, trying to get past the rancid smell of vampire until I got a firm hold on her scent.

I flew up the stairs and Toboe followed just like I knew he would.

* * *

In our search for Ava, we'd passed by at least three dozen dead vampires. Toboe and I didn't encounter anyone except for a few clueless guards that had probably been sired the night before. Newbie vamps were strong, but not exceptionally smart, especially if they hadn't undergone any training as to how to use their newfound abilities. We made quick work of them and continued on without much delay.

Ava had made it all the way to the sixty-fourth floor where the security department for the entire building was housed. We didn't meet any resistance up here and when I finally approached the main office for the head of security, the door was wide open. I sniffed the air, knowing that she was very close. I turned the corner and leaned against the doorframe, catching sight of my spirited mate casually sitting at the computer.

There was another vampire dead on the floor, finely dressed and clearly well off. He didn't look like he'd given her much of a fight. He'd probably underestimated the feisty little thing, but I knew better than to make that mistake myself. I cleared my throat and she just glanced in my direction for a moment before she turned back to the computer.

"The head of security, I take it," I said loudly, and she didn't even flinch. She didn't answer me either. She just kept typing. "What are you doing, little human?" I asked this time, addressing her directly although I was careful enough to keep my voice level. I wanted to know what she was up to before I put her in her place.

She didn't pause for even a second, but she lifted her arm and pointed a submachine gun right at me. She didn't look, but there was little doubt in my mind that if she pulled the trigger, she wouldn't miss her target. Her target being me.

Bad... *bad*... girl...

My palm twitched. I wanted to spank her. Hard.

"I thought you might come looking for me, so I brought a little something to make sure you thought twice before even thinking of touching me again. Every single round in this clip is silver-tipped, so I suggest you let me do my work in peace," she replied curtly.

The open challenge in her voice was hot as fuck. The more I was around her, the more I was impressed by her and the more I wanted to teach her a firm lesson at the end of my cock.

I stared at her, studying the way she held her weapon and seeing the experience behind it. She was wearing a bullet-proof vest, but underneath that she had a black tank top. I could see every line of muscle in her upper body. She was strong, but extraordinarily feminine and I found it to be extremely sexy.

The gun never wavered and neither did I.

I was pretty sure that she'd actually shoot me if I made any sudden movements, so I waited by the door. Patiently, I watched her typing one command after the next and before too long I was at least reasonably certain she was trying to guess a password so that she could get into their systems and find whatever information she was searching for.

Was she looking for information about her father?

Occasionally, she would glance my way, her face painted with fury and just the slightest hint of shame. Was she thinking about the way I forced her to come for me four times last night? Was she imagining how'd I'd torn her panties clean off and stuffed them in her mouth or how her virgin little body had gripped tightly at my cock as if her life depended on it?

Or maybe… just maybe she was thinking about my finger in her tight little bottom and wondering if my cock would hurt even more.

It would. No doubt about that. I was counting on it.

Out of pure curiosity, I sniffed the air.

Ahh…

Naughty little minx. She was wet. I could smell it.

I stared at her knowingly and her body language changed. She tensed slightly and met my gaze. She blushed before she managed to look away from me, but I'd seen the pretty pink hue all the same.

Was she challenging me on purpose?

She lifted her chin, glancing in my direction once again.

Oh, she was. She *wanted* her little bottom to get fucked.

Maybe she didn't believe that I'd follow through, but I'd always been a man of my word. Tonight would certainly be no different.

Toboe stood back behind me, watching the entire exchange. I could feel his amusement through the link we shared, probably because he'd never seen anyone train a gun on me and live to talk about it.

She stood up without pause and kept the gun trained on me as she rounded the desk. It didn't appear as if she found what she wanted or if she did, she wasn't saying anything about it. She didn't make any attempt to exit out of the door I was blocking, instead choosing to leave through a door at the side of the room. She opened the metal door and as it swung shut behind her, I could see a set of stairs going up.

My alarm bells started to ring.

From the plans I'd studied before, I knew she was headed somewhere exceedingly more dangerous than the rest of the tower. Above us was a two-story penthouse suite and I was certain that the head of the family resided there.

Shit.

This could get really bad.

I sprinted to the door and gripped the handle hard. It wouldn't turn. It was locked.

Instead of coming with me, Toboe went to the computer and chuckled softly at what he found.

"She set it up to lock behind her from the computer," he said. "I've gotta say, boss, you've got your hands full with this one."

"Can you disengage it from there?" I asked. I wasn't angry. It was clear that Ava was more than capable of looking after herself, even when it concerned the likes of me. I hadn't expected any less, but I was up for the challenge, nonetheless.

It would make her ultimate surrender that much sweeter when I took it for myself.

"We're going to have to use one of Genzo's techs. She set up a time-sensitive virus to make the computer unusable, which is already taking effect," he said thoughtfully.

Smart little thing.

"Pass me the bag. I'll take care of it," I offered, and he tossed the backpack full of Genzo's inventions to me without a moment's hesitation.

The door seemed to be operated by an eye scan but considering that she'd blown the head of security's head right off, that wasn't really an option. If anything, his bright red eyes were probably plastered somewhere on the wall with the rest of his unsightly purple brain matter.

I dug in the bag and pulled out a small unit. Carefully, I pressed it against the eye scanner and pulled my hand away before it passed a strong electrical current through it. It took several surges, but the unit eventually fizzled and powered off, leaving just the mechanics of the door to contend with.

Using another device, I scanned the wall for the electrical inputs that operated the lock itself. After a few minutes, the pinging changed pitch indicating that there was an electrical current just beneath it. I tore through the drywall like it was paper and ripped the wires right out. I shredded through the rest of the wall and pushed the deadbolt back into the door. It took every last bit of my strength, but when it finally slid back into place, I was able to pry the door open at last.

It had taken far longer than I'd wanted it to. I'd lost precious time. The head of the Venuti family was ancient and powerful. She could already be hurt or worse than that, she could be dead.

I had to get to her. Quickly.

Even if she did survive this, the ramifications of killing the kingpin of the Venuti family could be vast. If word spread that I was nearby, hell, it could even drag all the families into an all-out war. Hundreds of shifters could die, including several more from my pack. Humans could die too.

Whatever she had planned, I had to stop her and carry her out of here. I didn't care if I had to strip her and spank her ass bright red on the way out.

I sprinted up the stairs and Toboe's footsteps echoed behind me. I made it all the way to the top floor and when I burst out into the penthouse suite, I was horrified at the sight before my eyes.

There was a trail of dead guards leading to her. I dove into the room just in time to see her aiming her gun straight at the face of Nicolai, the head of the Venuti Clan.

"Ava, stop!" I called out.

She stilled, but she didn't lower the gun. Nicolai didn't move, which to his credit was smart of him.

"Lawson Clearwater," he acknowledged me, but he didn't take his eyes off the weapon in her hands. "Is this one your responsibility?"

"She is," I answered.

"The fuck I am," Ava spat.

"Ava," I warned, and I could have sworn I saw a glimmer of fear cross her face before her eyes glinted with fury. "Don't pull that trigger. Don't put that blood on your hands. Let me help you."

She didn't pull the trigger yet, and I was proud of her for it.

"If you kill him, you risk dragging all of the families into war. Vampire. Shifter. All of them. If that happens, people are going to die. Humans too," I warned her.

I was telling her the truth. She needed to know what would happen she pulled that trigger.

She glanced toward me quickly and a dark shadow glinted in her eyes. Her gaze held mine for a fraction of a second before she turned her head back toward Nicolai. Her mouth set in a grim line and immediately, it felt as if someone had dumped a bucket of ice water right over my head. The muscles in her hand tensed just the slightest bit as she squeezed the trigger, and I knew there was no way I would be able to reach her in time. I ran toward her anyway, but her aim was too true to stop what was already happening.

"I'm counting on it," she countered, and I watched in almost slow motion as the bullet burst out from the barrel of the gum, sailing through the air and hitting the head vampire directly between his eyes. Even though I'd seen it once before, the explosion of light was still as magnificent to behold as it was the first time. His head burst from within in a glorious display of blood and gore and I swore under my breath.

This was going to be really fucking complicated for me to fix.

I turned back toward her with a rising sense of frustration. She was going to pay for that. Dearly. I would make sure of it.

She reached for the gun loaded with silver bullets that she'd holstered at her waist, but I'd run out of patience. I rushed toward her. I didn't give her enough time to do anything more than wrap her fingers around the holster before I reached for her and stopped her from doing anything else.

I didn't say a word as I quickly grasped her wrist and twisted it just far enough to make her cry out with something that sounded like frustration or pain. I didn't much care which. I pushed it just a little bit further, just enough to remind her who was in control, and she finally relented and dropped the gun. It fell to the floor with a clatter. She tried to pull away and when that didn't work, she spun toward me. She drew her elbow back and threw it in a fairly well-executed attempt at hitting me with it in the face.

I was ready for her though. I knew she wouldn't go down without a fight.

Without pause, I gripped her around the waist and casually threw her over my shoulder. Toboe came up beside me and picked up the gun loaded with silver-tipped bullets. He tucked it into the waistband of his jeans. She wouldn't get it back.

Already familiar with the layout of the penthouse from my stolen blueprints, I exited the room filled with carnage and went off down the hall until I found Nicolai's office. He wasn't going to be needing it now, but I most certainly did.

It was a corner office with floor-to-ceiling windows. The lights were off, but they weren't going to stay that way for long. Set in the center of the room was a grand desk made of luxurious cherry wood and I eyed it. It would be perfect for what she had coming.

"Find the lights, Toboe. I want to make sure the entire city sees what happens to naughty little mates who ignore their alpha's instructions," I demanded.

She furiously pummeled her fists into my back. I could hardly feel it. She kicked and squirmed over my shoulder, but it didn't matter now. I'd gotten my hands on her and it was about time I truly taught her who was in charge. I'd granted her mercy last night, but she didn't need that. She needed my ruthless control, and she was going to get it.

I'd start with my belt.

The lights clicked on, illuminating the room and exposing us to whomever happened to look up at the penthouse suite of the Venuti tower from down below.

"Barricade the door. I have need of this room and although I'm fairly certain there isn't anyone left to attack us thanks to my little vampire hunter here, I don't want to be disturbed," I barked. Ava's struggles began anew. She started to scream and call me a number of names. I paid her no mind. She could say whatever she wanted right now.

Before the night was through though, she was going to be screaming my name and begging for mercy.

"Let me go," she shrieked.

"I made you a promise last night, little mate and I intend to keep it. The only thing up to you now is how long it will take you to beg me for it."

My cock was already rock hard.

She was in for a very long night.

CHAPTER 5

Ava

When I'd first seen him, my clit had pulsed with desire. I'd done my best to hide it and keep myself calm, but images from the night before came rushing back with wild abandon. I'd tried to swallow all of it, but there was a part of me that wanted to feel his hands on me again.

But this...

This was not exactly what I'd had in mind.

The goddamn fucking bastard had no right.

I'd given his men the slip early this evening and I had made it all the way inside the tower looking for information by myself. I'd searched everything on the security head's computer after I'd blasted his head off, but I'd found nothing that would connect my father and the Venuti other than camera evidence of him entering the building on three separate occasions. That wasn't enough. I needed more than that.

I needed names. Contracts. Something. Anything really. I still had so many questions and none of them had been answered even though I'd made it this far. I had a hunch that there would be something in the kingpin's penthouse, maybe on his computer or maybe there was a physical paper trail in a records room up here somewhere, but I needed to get searching before any more of the vampires showed up.

I was getting dangerously low on my sunfire bullet supplies. There had been more guards posted inside the building than I had anticipated.

"Release me, you prick! I don't have time for this," I yelled.

"You're going to make time, little human," he scowled, and I pounded my fists against his back. With me still draped over his shoulder, he swept his arm across the surface of the desk, clearing off more than half of it. The rustle of crinkled papers was deafening, but it was masked by the pounding of my blood rushing to my ears. I shrieked with fury as he tossed me face down against the wooden surface. Immediately, I pushed my hands against the top of the desk, intending to spin around and punch him in the face, but his palm firmly slammed against my upper back, stopping me before I could get any leverage whatsoever.

"Toboe, meet Ava. My mate," he continued.

"I'm not your mate, asshole. Let me go!" I yelled. I reached back and tried to swing at him, but he captured my wrist and pinned it behind my waist. No matter how much I twisted and turned my arm, I couldn't break free. His grasp held tight.

Shit.

This wasn't good.

For the first time that night, fear flickered deep inside me, forcing me to reevaluate the situation I'd gotten myself into.

I'd made all the preparations in the world to deal with Lawson if he happened to make an appearance tonight, but still he had managed to put me at a disadvantage. I struggled as much as I could, but it was all in vain. Just like before, he subdued me with just his strength alone.

He reached down and pulled off my combat boots one by one. I tried to kick him in the face, but he seemed like he was ready for that too. Without even a moment of hesitation, he reached around my waist and unbuttoned my black jeans. He was so rough that I heard the button pop free. It clicked quietly when it bounced off the hardwood floor beneath me. He jerked my pants down and the zipper broke, but I doubted he very much cared.

I renewed my efforts to escape him as he exposed my panty-clad bottom and my thighs. He left my jeans pulled down to just below my knees and when I tried to kick them off, I only succeeded in tangling them around my ankles. He chuckled and my face reddened, whether with fury or with shame, I wasn't sure. I tried not to think about the reason why.

"I think I'll leave those just how they are," he mused and a string of expletives that would have made a sailor blush flew off my lips. I slapped my free hand against the desk and tried to push up. I screeched with anger when I didn't move even a single inch.

I could do one-handed pushups, for Christ's sake. I should be able to do this.

"Let me up, motherfucker!" I yelled.

He ignored me, refusing to acknowledge a word I said.

Instead, he just gripped my panties in his fingers. I halfway expected him to pull them down just like he had my jeans, but he didn't.

He tore them clean off.

I should have known he would. Every single word died on my lips as a piercing volley of agony blossomed across my pussy. The fabric didn't tear as easily as the ones he torn from me last night, which meant it hurt far more this time. He wrenched them from in between my thighs, pinching my folds and scraping against my clit hard. I tried to breathe through the pain. There was no fighting it. There was only surviving its terrible sting. I prayed for it to lessen and when it finally did, I just closed my eyes and sighed in relief.

"Would you like to continue?" he asked purposefully.

"No," I squeaked, still trembling from the aching soreness in between my thighs.

I swallowed hard, trying to cope with the residual pain. There had to be a better way to handle this. Showing him my fury at his heavy-handedness hadn't gotten me anywhere, simply earning myself a very sore pussy as a result. I closed my eyes and just focused on pulling air in and out of my lungs.

"Good," he murmured, and my muscles tightened with restrained fear.

There was something about his tone that made me hold my tongue. There wasn't even a sliver of gentleness hidden in his words, nothing that spoke to the man I'd seen yesterday, the one who had held me and comforted me after he was through with me. He didn't address me with anger or even frustration, but with a measured even calm tone that felt far more dangerous. Every word of defiance that I'd planned to utter died on my lips and I chewed the inside of my cheek. I settled on a new tactic.

"Lawson. Wait. Please," I began, ensuring to keep my voice quieter and softer, hoping to appeal to his gentler side before it was too late. "Please. You have to let me up. I need to search Nicolai's computer before the rest of the vampire clan find out the tower has been compromised. I need information and I know it's somewhere in this penthouse. So please, I'm asking you to let me up so I can finish what I came here to do."

"You're going to have to wait, little one. You're in need of a hard lesson first," he warned, and I stilled.

Dammit. Consider that strategy dead in the water.

"I won't allow it," I spat angrily, and he cleared his throat.

"I don't think you quite understand the gravity of what you've done, little mate. This is my city, and it is my responsibility to deal with the ramifications of your impulsive decision to pursue vengeance or whatever this is. More important though, it is my duty to see to it that you are punished for it," he declared, and I struggled in his hold.

"You have no right," I sputtered.

"I have every right, little human. Not only have you killed dozens of members of the Venuti clan, but you've murdered the head of it. Maybe you hadn't realized it, but the tower was manned by a skeleton crew. There's more of them hidden away somewhere. I don't know where yet, but I'm going to have to find out. You see, Nicolai has family, vampires he's sired that have been groomed for centuries to take over in his place should the need ever arise. They're going to want answers and if they don't get what they want, it's going to end badly, especially when they find out it was you that did all of it," he scolded.

I pressed my lips together.

I knew the Venuti had something to do with my father's death. If I couldn't find the answers I needed here, I would find them eventually.

"If you had just answered my questions last night, I could have helped you. You didn't have to resort something like this to find whatever you're searching for, mate," he continued softly.

"I did what I had to do," I scoffed. He simply didn't understand. This was more than just a quest for vengeance. I needed to do this to clear my family name. I needed to know my father hadn't just cracked and turned into a monster that day.

I needed to know. For me.

"In my world, impulsiveness is not something I can allow. I need answers and you're going to give them to me," he demanded, and I struggled against him.

"I won't tell you anything," I yelled.

"I've run out of patience, little human. You will tell me everything," he snarled.

"Do your worst," I said as courageously as I could. He chuckled softly and that twinge of fear deep in the pit of my stomach magnified tenfold.

The sound of him pulling his belt from the loops of his pants echoed all around me and I stilled. With my bottom entirely bare and on display over the massive desk, his intentions soon became all too clear.

The first time the belt slapped against my skin was a shock. It was far louder than I expected and that caught me off guard, but the line of fire that followed quickly grasped my full attention. It felt warm at first, then blazing hot and the eventual burning sting made me rise up on the tips of my toes as I tried to take it.

The second and third followed in quick succession, cruelly punishing and painfully harsh.

I hadn't realized how deadly serious Lawson had been before.

I did now.

The fiery lash of the belt was like a vicious brand on my naked backside. I tried to use my one arm to push up against the desk so that I could escape him and run, but with one arm he held both my wrist and my body firmly in place. I gave it everything I had, but it was as if I was doing nothing at all. He was far too strong, his species far more powerful than a simple human like me.

"Wait!" I cried out.

He didn't.

The belt thrashed against my bottom, over and over. He kicked my feet open wide and the end of the belt clipped the area in between my cheeks, causing me to cry out from the intensity of the extremely harsh sting that followed. Despite all of that though, my bare pussy was wet and exposed and as the belt rained down, a terrifying realization dawned on me.

The belt could hit between my thighs too and I was so very ashamed that the thought of that was making me even wetter.

As a measure of self-preservation, I attempted to press my legs back together so that I could hide my most vulnerable flesh, but he swiftly kicked my feet apart. He deliberately swung the belt between my legs, swatting my pussy with the flat of the leather hard enough to silently warn me to keep still. I froze, fearful and desperately aroused.

What was wrong with me? Why was the thought of him hurting me like this turning me on?

I'd told myself that last night had been a fluke. I'd vowed to never let it happen again, but here I was wet for him once more. Wanting him. Needing him. I was doing everything I'd swore I wouldn't do again. I couldn't stop myself. I was caught in a red haze of arousal and my head couldn't work my way out of it.

I was caught up in the idea of him.

I hadn't been able to stop thinking about him all day. I couldn't forget the way my body had gripped the length of his cock. The feel of him surging in and out of me roughly enough to leave my pussy quite sore long after he was through with me had been on my mind all day. With every step, I'd felt him between my thighs just like he promised.

I don't know why, but I *liked* that.

There was something else he'd said he'd do too. Something even more forbidden. Something filthy and dirty and wrong. That didn't stop me from wanting that as well.

Why?

My thighs trembled and my pussy clenched hard in anticipation.

"You will keep your legs open. If I have to make you, I'll be forced to turn this little pussy bright red with my belt," he demanded.

I obeyed and I didn't understand why.

I cried out and the belt lashed against my backside once again with brutal force. He whipped the tops of my cheeks, and I clenched them, but that only made the pain that much worse. The belt descended lower and lower until the only thing it was punishing was the backs of my thighs. With a concerted amount of effort, I forced myself to relax and take whatever he gave me, but it was so very hard.

I pressed my lips together, determined to show him that I could be strong and make it through whatever he intended to inflict. The belt was so much worse than his hand had been however, and it took everything in me to keep my lips shut. I bit the inside of my cheek, desperately trying to keep myself quiet. I bit hard enough to taste blood.

I vowed that he wouldn't break me.

As if he could read my thoughts, he whipped me harder and the first real cry of distress fled my lips. I struggled beneath him, and Lawson cleared his throat. The sound of it made me nervous.

"Take her hands, Toboe," he murmured. "Ava, I want you to meet my beta. He is my second in command."

Without ceremony, the man who had entered the room with him rounded the desk and grasped my wrists in his strong hands. Lawson's palm flattened on my back, holding me even more firmly than before. I tried to twist my hands out of the beta's clutches, but I was at such a disadvantage that it did absolutely nothing at all.

I was trapped and just when I thought the belting couldn't get any harder, it did. It got so much worse. I tried to arch into each lash and that did nothing. My legs pressed together involuntarily even though I tried to keep them apart. He growled in warning and through sheer force of will, I slid my right foot to the side a few inches.

"Good girl," he purred.

I don't know why, but those two words settled me.

The belt thrashed my bare bottom so thoroughly that I knew I would be sore for a long time after he was through with me. My bottom cheeks burned, and my thighs felt like they'd been scalded with boiling hot water. For the first time, I began to feel regret. Maybe if I had waited, maybe if I'd spent more time trying to figure out who Lawson was, I could have figured out just how much power he wielded over the quarter. Maybe he could have helped me get the answers I was looking for.

"Please. I'm sorry," I pleaded.

My vow to be quiet had long fled. Each lash flared hot against my skin and when several descended even lower on my thighs, my eyes began to water.

I didn't want to cry.

"Please," I begged. My fingernails scratched against the wood beneath me, and a hard shudder raced down my spine.

There was nothing I could think of other than the punishing leather of his belt.

One lash.

Pain.

Another.

Agony.

The first sob pitched me forward and a single tear dripped down my cheek. More followed and soon, there was a tiny puddle pooling beneath my chin.

I broke for him, and I broke hard.

In that moment, I knew that I was his. I'd denied it before, but I couldn't anymore. All I wanted was to feel my body against his. I wanted his arms around me.

The metal clasp of his belt clinked against the wooden desk, but I was crying too hard to really notice. Toboe's fingers relaxed around my wrists as did Lawson's on my back.

"Shhh. It's alright, little mate," he murmured softly.

His arms were suddenly around me, lifting me off the desk and cradling me within them. He sat down in one of the massive leather armchairs that were set in front of the grand desk and pulled me into his lap. I wasn't certain why, but I clutched at him as if he was a lifeline, as if I'd fall into pieces if I ever let go. I nestled my face into his shoulder, breathing in his scent and trying to stop myself from crying.

"Such a good girl," he purred.

There it was again. Those two words that made my heart flutter and my pussy flood with heat.

His arms closed around me even tighter and the feeling of his body on mine was more than I could handle. The tip of my nose brushed against his throat as his fingers grazed beneath my chin. With a single finger, he lifted my gaze to meet his.

My eyes searched his and I chewed my lip, feeling unsure and unsteady, but it turned out that didn't matter. He pressed his mouth to mine, his kiss possessive and wanting and entirely in control. My hand ventured up the hard lines of his chest as his tongue tangled with my own and I lost myself in everything that was him.

His scent.

His love.

The way he'd punished me and rewarded me with his kiss.

His hand slipped between my thighs, and I sucked in a shaky breath. My clit pulsed hard, and a soft whine escaped me.

His belt had been vicious across my bare bottom and the backs of my thighs felt more than a little marked from it, but the rest of me was burning up inside with need and it only grew hotter the more I thought about it. He cupped my pussy gently and rubbed the pads of his fingers between my wet folds, finding my clit and teasing it just hard enough to make me squirm against him. His touch turned more persistent, firmer and then he drew back just enough so that he could slide one finger inside me.

"My, my, little mate. You're soaking wet for me, aren't you?" he asked.

I blushed at his observation. He was right. I was so very wet right now and I couldn't deny the fact that it was all his fault. His dominance over me had awakened something deep inside me, a need I hadn't known was there. That knowledge ensured I would never be the same again.

"I expect an answer, little one," he coaxed, and he pumped that single digit in and out of me. He moved slowly, like he was taunting me with the pleasure that I knew his finger was capable of.

"Yes," I squeaked, feeling my face redden even further.

"When you're being punished, little mate, you will refer to me as your alpha. Now answer me properly, or you'll go over my knee," he demanded softly.

I chewed my lip, and he used his thumb to wipe away a stray tear from my cheek.

There it was. The gentleness I'd seen just last night.

I swallowed heavily.

"Yes, alpha," I whispered. I stared back at him, feeling so unsure of myself. My fingers trembled and I pressed them against my thighs.

He smiled and his eyes sparkled with pride.

"Good girl," he murmured, and my clit pulsed with desire at his praise.

Yesterday, we'd felt like strangers. Today, he was looking at me like I was his lover and I liked that.

"We're going to have to take care of this soaking wet little pussy, aren't we, my pretty mate?"

"You keep calling me that. I'm not even a wolf. How can I possibly be your mate?" I asked. I didn't intend to be rebellious or anything of the sort. I was just curious, and his eyes glinted with a sudden fierce possessiveness that made my heart flutter with hope that maybe he could feel something like what I was beginning to feel too.

His hand returned to its place between my thighs, and I sucked in an aroused breath.

ALPHA KING

"Do you think an alpha cannot recognize his one true mate, little one? You and I are fated for each other. You fight me with that beautifully fierce mind, but your body already knows that we are meant for one another. Your nipples are hard and begging for me to kiss them. Even now, your eyes are dilated, your shoulders are bowing toward me, and even though your bottom bears the mark of my belt, you're soaking wet for me. You need me to take you. I am your mate, and your body knows that I am your alpha. It is only a matter of time before the rest of you follows," he explained and with every word, he slid his fingertip up and down my clit.

I felt like I was on fire.

"You're mine, my pretty mate and I don't plan on letting you go. Not now. Not ever. You're mine for always and I intend to show you exactly what that means starting tonight."

My pussy clenched down hard. What exactly did he mean?

"Look at me, little mate," he said quietly.

I obeyed, trying to grapple with the way my stomach was tightening with anxious arousal.

"Tell me, little mate. What was on your mind when you woke up this morning? What did you think of when you felt the soreness between your thighs? What was the image in your head when you felt that ache between your legs with each and every step you took today?"

I whimpered with shame. I closed my eyes, too embarrassed to meet his eyes anymore.

"No. Don't hide from me. Open your eyes," he commanded.

His instruction blossomed over me, and I suddenly found myself wanting to do as he asked. I wanted to please him and that terrified me as much as it aroused me.

I realized it was more than a simple want after a moment.

It was a need. I *needed* to obey him.

I opened my eyes, and I felt my cheeks flush bright pink at the same time that my pussy clenched down tight. A trickle of my own arousal dripped down the expanse of my right inner thigh and my blush deepened at the feeling of it.

"Your cock, alpha," I whined softly.

"Were you thinking of my cock fucking you, sweet mate?" he pressed.

"Yes, alpha," I whispered, feeling my face flush even more deeply.

"In which of your pretty holes were you thinking about my cock, little mate?"

I blanched, a soft cry of mortification escaping me.

I had hoped he wouldn't ask that. I'd hoped to keep that hidden from him.

I could say my mouth or my pussy, but that would be a lie and I didn't want to lie to him. I turned away, too overwhelmed in my shame, but he captured my chin and forced me to look back at him. His fingers flattened and I knew that waiting much longer would test his patience and likely earn me more of his belt.

"In my bottom, alpha," I finally answered, my voice shaking with every syllable.

"You were thinking about my promise, weren't you?" he asked. His finger slid backwards from my pussy, only just settling over top of my bottom hole. I remembered how he'd forced that same finger inside me last night, how painful it felt, but that wasn't all.

As punishing as it had been, it had made me feel curious.

I wanted to know more. I wanted to know what it was like.

"Yes, alpha," I whispered, my voice hardly audible.

"Stand up for me, little mate," he murmured.

I stood up on shaky legs. I almost lost my balance once and his arms swept around my waist, catching me and holding me steady so that I didn't fall. I gripped his forearm with my fingers hard enough that my knuckles turned white. I released him almost as quickly as I had grabbed him.

I didn't want to hurt him, which was quite silly when I thought about how very sore my backside was from his belt.

"Go and bend over the desk for me. Show me that needy little pussy and I might just decide to reward you," he whispered gruffly.

I whimpered loudly—with need, with desire, with nervousness, I didn't know.

His command flowed over me like a warm waterfall. It was like a soft tingle across the expanse of my skin, a quiet prickling of a magical link between us that seemed to grow stronger the longer I was with him.

I took a hesitant step toward the desk and then another and another. When I reached it, I slowly slid the tips of my fingers against its cool surface, trying to will at least a little bravery from somewhere deep inside me to come forth.

"Do I need to bend you over the desk myself, Ava?" he asked quietly, a subtle threat laced into every syllable.

"No, alpha," I whispered quickly and that was more than enough to make me follow his instructions. I didn't try to hide myself this time. I bent over the desk and spread my legs, putting my own body on display for him this time.

He stood up and even though I wasn't facing him, I knew that he was looking at me. I could feel his gaze on my skin, hot and smoldering and beautifully possessive. He didn't touch me for the longest time and every second that he made me wait made my arousal amplify tenfold. When he finally brushed the rough pads of his fingers against my skin, I shuddered with need and a soft cry emerged from my throat that sounded deceptively like a moan and a whine combined.

It spoke to the quiet desperation surging through my veins.

I wanted his cock.

Badly.

I arched my back and I slowly realized something about myself.

I didn't want him to ask either. I just wanted him to take me. Hard. Rough. Like the savage beast I knew him to be.

I didn't need a man.

I needed a monster.

I needed *him*.

His fingers slipped in between my thighs, and I knew I was even more drenched than I was when I'd left the safety of his arms.

"Little mate…" he purred.

He didn't have to say it. I knew it.

I heard the sound of his zipper and a shudder raced down my spine. I gasped when the heat of his cock pressed up against my entrance, and I whined when he thrust every last inch of his cock inside me in the following seconds. I could still feel the remaining soreness from last night in his rough claiming of my pussy, but that only added even more fuel to the fire.

He slammed into me several times and I cried out with pleasure. My inner walls gripped tightly around him as his pelvis slapped against the sore welts on my backside. Without thinking, I arched into his thrusts, and he clicked his tongue in disapproval. Slowly, he slipped his cock from my pussy and replaced it with two of his fingers.

He took those thick digits and thoroughly coated them with my wetness before he pulled them free and tapped them against my bottom hole.

"I taught you a lesson with my belt, didn't I, little mate?" he asked dangerously.

"Yes, alpha," I answered, my voice wavering and my pussy clenching with needy fear.

"I'm going to teach you a lesson with my cock next, sweet girl," he warned and just when I felt my stomach pitch forward anxiously, he pushed both fingers roughly into my bottom. I wasn't ready so there was no time to clench or try to keep him out, catching me off guard and unprepared. I keened with the stretching burn as it billowed outward from my bottom hole, radiating up and down my spine and consuming me with its deliciously terrible pain.

He pumped those fingers in and out of me, dragging out that scorching ache as long as possible and I shivered hard beneath him. Eventually, the pain started to ebb away and the sheer power of the mind-rending pleasure that followed blew me out of the water.

"In a moment, I'm going to replace my fingers with my cock, little girl. I want you to think about that as I use them to stretch this tight little hole wide enough so that I can fuck it," he demanded, and I shivered hard.

"Please, alpha," I pleaded. I was no longer certain of what I was pleading for, just that I wanted more of whatever this was.

I could feel every knuckle slipping in and out of my bottom, over and over again. Thick. Rough. Painfully decadent.

My bottom tightened as I imagined what his cock might feel like instead of his fingers and my legs trembled a bit in anticipation. I chewed my lip, my clit throbbing hard, and I moaned, arching my back and taking him a bit deeper inside me with every thrust.

I couldn't stop thinking about what was to come and when he pulled his hand free from my bottom, I sucked in a breath as a combination of fear and arousal twisted me from the inside out. My muscles tensed as he slipped his cock back inside my pussy, using my ample wetness to coat himself. I clenched all around him, enjoying the painful edge of pleasure as he used me as roughly as he pleased.

But then, he pulled his cock free of me and pressed it against my already sore bottom hole. I tensed with anxiety as his palm pressed against my lower back, forcing me against the desk just as he had done when he'd spanked me.

I suddenly found myself overwhelmed with the thought of how much this was going to hurt. Anxiously, I pressed my palms against the desk and tried to get up. He didn't let me.

"I told you I was going to punish you with my cock, didn't I?" he warned.

The tip of his cock breached my bottom hole and I gasped when he stilled. My muscles tightened around him, and a fierce scorching pain radiated through me. It intensified further and I cried out, suddenly far more nervous than I had been before.

"Yes, alpha," I whimpered.

"I'm going to use this beautiful little hole and it's going to hurt, sweet mate. If you're very good, I might just allow you to come for me," he warned and he thrust himself a bit further inside me, causing me to gasp at the roughness of it.

A strangled whine escaped me, and I bit my lower lip, trying to keep quiet as much as I could.

I focused on his words and my clit pulsed hard. With a sudden forceful thrust, he slammed the rest of his cock inside my bottom, reawakening the sizzling burn for several long seconds before it faded into a gentler pulsing soreness.

At least until he started to fuck me.

"Your bottom is so very tight, mate. I'm really going to enjoy this," he said darkly, and my muscles clenched down hard all around him.

"Please don't," I begged.

"You should know that no matter how much you beg, this is only going to end with my seed dripping from this tight little hole," he answered, and a hot shiver of desire sliced through me to the core.

His fingers wound around my hips and pulled me back from the desk just far enough so that he could reach underneath me. His fingertips ventured down just enough to capture my clit, circling it slowly as he pumped in and out of my ass.

A hard jolt of pleasure raced through me, and I couldn't contain myself any longer.

"Oh," I moaned, unable to keep quiet.

He pounded into my bottom, using me as hard as he wanted and despite the punishing agony that came with it, my desire continued to grow. The more it hurt, the more I wanted to come with him fucking me like this.

The more I craved it.

"Oh, sweet mate. I could fuck this little bottom all night," he mused, and I whined nervously. I already knew he had more stamina than I did, so it worried me that he was speaking the truth.

"Please," I pleaded.

"Does it make you blush to know that you were wet enough that I didn't even need lubricant to take your virgin ass?" he asked, fucking me hard enough so that I could hear it. It was embarrassingly loud, and I blushed hard, knowing that everything he said was absolutely correct.

I'd been so wet that his entry had been almost easy.

"Your body recognizes me as your alpha, little one. By the time I'm through with this naughty hole, you will understand that completely," he groaned.

His fingers danced over top of my clit, and I pressed back against him, earning myself a deeper fucking than before. As if he was rewarding me, he pressed more firmly against my needy bud, forcing me higher toward the edge of bliss.

"You're going to come for me three times with my cock in your ass, little mate. I want them each long and hard," he demanded, and I shivered hard.

"Yes, alpha," I whimpered.

My legs shook and my inner thighs squeezed tight. He kicked my feet open a bit wider, forcing me to spread for him and in turn, his cock pushed into me further than ever. It felt filthy and wrong and entirely too right.

"Please, I need…" I begged.

I felt like I was on a rollercoaster, climbing higher and higher until I coasted over the peak of a massive drop. I knew whatever happened next would change me, but I knew that he would be there to catch me once I fell.

"I know, sweet girl. Come for me. I want to feel you tighten around my cock as you scream my name," he purred.

My impending orgasm felt so much deeper, so much more powerful than anything I'd ever felt before. His fingers pressed even more firmly against my clit, rubbing over top of it with such vigor that I knew following his instructions would be simple.

I was going to come.

And it was going to be hard.

"Come, sweet mate," he demanded.

I couldn't fight it any longer. I gave into my desire. I gave into him.

I gave into my fate.

My orgasm started in the center of my core, twisting hard and spiraling down to the tips of my toes and the edges of my fingers. For several long moments, I knew nothing but the blinding white heat of ecstasy surging through me, destroying me from within.

I screamed as my body clenched down tight, pleasure and pain coming together in an intoxicating mix that left me reeling. My legs quivered and I was suddenly grateful for the desk underneath me that was holding me up.

I knew I wouldn't be able to stand if it wasn't there.

He didn't slow down. Not even once.

"That's it, mate. Tighten that bottom around my cock," he demanded, and my body instantly responded to his command.

As my orgasm faded, my fucking began to grow more painful. I dug my fingers into the desk and whined softly, trying to take the increasing burn as the seconds passed.

"Did you enjoy that orgasm, little mate? Is it beginning to hurt now?" he purred.

I moaned, but it sounded like a mixture of pain and desire, neither one stronger than the other.

He was right.

"Yes, alpha," I whimpered.

That only resulted in him fucking me harder. His fingers gripped my hip hard enough that I knew they'd probably leave a mark, but for some reason, I liked that.

I would like his fingerprints on my hips, and I would enjoy the marks of his belt on my ass even more.

I felt myself falling again, edging closer toward a second orgasm. It was as if I was a train about to hurtle off its tracks. Nothing could stop what was coming, not even me.

His fingers worked my clit so roughly that I knew I would be sore there too after he was done. His cock thrust in and out of my bottom and I keened, struggling against my release even though I knew it was inevitable.

He'd said he was going to make me come three times and I knew he was going to follow through with that.

That made tonight even more terrifying than yesterday. It made it even more real. Which in turn resulted in turning me on that much more.

I screamed and my legs began to shake. My orgasm was upon me before I was ready for it, white-hot bliss than shook me with the force of an earthquake. Every muscle in my body tensed tight and I lost control of everything.

I writhed beneath him, arching into his thrusts while rubbing my clit roughly against his fingers. There was no more thought behind my actions. I thrashed. I moaned. I behaved like a wanton little whore, and I came even harder because of it.

My orgasm seemingly lasted forever, and I suffered through every last second of it. I suffered through an addicting mix of sensations.

Fear.

Bliss.

Stunning agony.

It was the most fulfilling thing I'd ever experienced in my life.

He released my hip and slipped his hand around the front of my throat, cupping it and lifting me so that my back was flush against his chest. He never stopped fucking me, but I felt him kiss the back of my head and I practically melted in his arms.

As my second release began to fade, he groaned in my ear and a delicious shiver of desire raced down my spine.

"You've got one orgasm left before I finish with you, little mate," he snarled, and I whined in nervous anticipation.

"I don't think I can," I said nervously.

"You will. It's only a matter of time," he growled, and my core clamped down hard. He used the flats of three fingers to punish my clit. I shuddered against him and begged him for relief, but he didn't listen.

He just kept forcing my pleasure forth anyway.

Soon enough, I was writhing with need as his cock punished my bottom hole hard. He fucked me so hard that his pelvis slapped against my bottom cheeks, reawakening the burning welts his belt had left behind.

I knew before this was over that I would be sore inside and out.

I keened, struggling to take what he gave me even though I could do nothing but accept it.

He groaned in my ear, and I felt his cock throb deep inside my bottom. His fingers worried my clit roughly and I knew my third orgasm was close.

"Oh, please!" I pleaded.

"Come, sweet mate. Come hard for me," he coaxed, and I screamed as his words quaked through me.

I closed my eyes and I shattered on his cock.

Exquisite ecstasy reigned free within me, surging through me like a tidal wave as he held me close against him. His cock pulsed hard, and I closed my eyes, allowing myself just to feel.

The first blazing pulse of his seed surged inside me, and my bliss took over everything in me. It destroyed me.

Every muscle tensed. My eyes watered and tears began to drip down my cheeks. Nothing could have readied me for such a powerful experience and through it all, his cum continued to burn and mark me deep inside my ass. My fucking never slowed and just when I thought I was going to break into pieces, my eyes rolled back in my head and my whole body began to shake. His arms wrapped around me and lifted me clear of the floor, leaving me suspended in the air on top of his cock.

I shook so hard I began to sob.

"I'm sorry, alpha," I whispered and still, my body shook with pleasure and pain. I was lost in the bliss he'd forced on me and when it finally ebbed into a manageable pulse, I sagged against him, thoroughly broken and used.

"Shhh… That's my good girl," he murmured, but that didn't stop my tears. Gently, he pulled free of my bottom and gathered me in his lap. My breath hitched in my throat again and again as I cried. He took my arms and placed them around his neck, allowing me to clutch him and I adored him for it.

Right now, he was my safe space. He'd broken me and I knew he would put me back together again.

His palm cupped the back of my head. Gently, he pulled back and kissed the trails of tears that lined my cheeks and I melted for him.

"I'm sorry," I murmured again, not knowing what else to say.

"I forgave you the moment you pulled that trigger, sweet mate," he reassured me.

"But the war," I began anxiously, and he shook his head.

"Whatever comes our way now, we will deal with together. Do you understand, mate?" he pressed, and I nodded. "I will protect you. You have my word."

I took a deep breath and he pulled me into a sweet kiss that left me reeling and breathlessly needy for the man who had just punished me.

"We're going to talk now, Ava. I want you to tell me everything," he coaxed, and I stared into his eyes for a long time.

All my life, I'd trained to fight against monsters like him. I prepared for them to try to kill me for the things I knew. My father had warned me of them, of all of them, but maybe he'd never met one like Lawson. I'd never imagined that I would consider working with one of them, let alone spreading my legs for one.

But here I was considering doing both.

My pussy clenched tight.

"You'll protect me?" I asked softly.

"You're mine now, Ava. I protect what's mine," he snarled. "I promise you that. You already know I'm a man of my word, my pretty mate," he added as he stared into my eyes, not breaking for even a moment.

"What does it mean to be your mate?" I asked.

"It means you're my everything, Ava. That I'm never going to have eyes for another. It means that if you run from me, I will find you. If you disobey me, I will punish you, but above all else, I will love you with all that I have to give," he vowed.

"Do you really mean that?" I asked.

I'd never heard any man talk like that before, except in the movies and romance novels. If it hadn't been him who said it, I wouldn't have believed it.

"I mean every single word, sweet girl. Now tell me everything, before I decide to take you over my knee for another lesson in obeying your alpha," he warned gently.

I knew I'd pushed him far enough. Anyone else would have probably killed me for what I'd done today, but not him.

I licked my lips and nodded, adjusting my knees to either side of his waist so I was facing him. I wanted to see him for what I was about to say.

"I've never told anyone what I'm about to tell you," I whispered softly, glancing at his beta at the door. I blushed softly, knowing he'd seen everything that my alpha had just done to me as punishment. All of my shame. Everything. I swallowed hard, chewing at my lip.

"I trust Toboe with my life. You can speak freely when he's here at my side," he said, likely sensing my hesitation.

"Have you heard of the name Ethan Winters?" I asked tentatively.

He nodded.

"So, you know of what happened here in the quarter?" My voice shook a bit more. I closed my eyes as the footage flashed in my head once more and I looked away from him.

The gunfire popped in my ear, as if it were real and not just a fragmented memory.

"I do. As one of the reigning leaders that rule this city, it is my job to know, especially when it happens in my own territory," he answered firmly.

I took a deep breath and licked my lips.

"You see, that wasn't like him. He used to be a respected professor in his industry before he left the public sector to begin pursuing consulting work instead. He worked for some of the most powerful shifters and vampires in the world. I never knew their names or the details of the contracts that he took, but he did teach me enough so that I could protect myself. Since I was a young girl, I've trained hard to be able to stand against your kind. I've learned how to make weapons like the silver-tipped bullets or even the sunfire ones, or something as simple as carving a wooden stake," I began.

"It's rare for a human to know we exist," he said softly, studying my face as he did so.

"I know," I murmured, and I chewed my lip.

"What else, pretty mate?" he coaxed.

With a heavy sigh, everything else fell out of me. I told him what I found on the head of security's computer, that my father had only just mentioned the Venuti family name once in passing and that I was sure that they had something to do with the circumstances surrounding his death. Lawson listened quietly and attentively. He just let me talk while his fingers traced up and down my thighs. When I finished, I gazed at him, feeling almost anxious to hear what he had to say.

He brushed a stray lock of hair behind my head and smiled.

"I understand why you fought me so hard, Ava," he told me. "You want to protect your family name. Loyalty is an honorable thing and that is something I can respect. I'm proud of you, little mate."

I breathed a sigh of relief.

"Tomorrow, I will introduce you to the members of my pack. I can't replace the family you lost, but as my mate you will come to understand that you will be welcomed with open arms into another," he added.

"Yes, alpha," I whispered, at a loss to say anything else.

"Now, let us find the evidence you were looking for. Together."

CHAPTER 6

Ava

I searched his eyes, trying to look for some trick or other alternative motive within those green and yellow depths, but I found none. With trepidation, I took his hand when he offered it, sliding my fingertips across his. The feeling of his skin against mine was like a breath of fresh air and I sighed softly in relief.

It felt safe.

Maybe it was. Maybe I should take that last leap of faith and give him my heart.

Gently, he lifted me off of his lap and set me down on my feet. With a guiding hand on my lower back, he led me around the desk so that I could sit down in Nicolai's chair. He leaned against the desk next to me, watching as my trembling fingers reached for the mouse and keyboard. I was still very much aware that I was naked from the waist down, but I didn't let it slow me down.

I clicked and the screen lit up. I was surprised to see it open straight to the desktop. There was a pretty Italian landscape set as the background, but other than that, it was pretty much as you would expect a normal office computer to look like rather than one owned by the head of a notorious vampire crime family. It was really quite striking in its normalcy.

I expected a password window, but there wasn't one. In fact, there really wasn't any sort of protection whatsoever. Maybe Nicolai had been arrogant enough to think that his enemies would never make it past his security guards and as a result, his files were just all out in the open.

I still felt emotionally raw, but his cockiness elicited the smallest chuckle from my lips.

Stupid bastard.

"I don't even have to hack it to get in," I grinned.

"Apparently, he hadn't thought to protect himself from the likes of you," Lawson muttered, his amused laugh bouncing all around me.

"There's a firewall meant to keep everyone outside this building out of their network, but it doesn't do any good for those of us already inside," I observed, smirking a bit at the Venuti's cockiness.

I opened a few folders, glancing over the records of the building, the hotel revenue, the wait staff that serviced the lower levels. It was all pretty much run of the mill, at least until I stumbled on a Venuti Clan family tree.

They were so much bigger than I imagined. There were names listed from the 1400s and some that dated even earlier than that. There were a few men and women so old that the date wasn't even recorded, and someone had simply written down an estimated range instead. I chewed my lip and I zoomed out a bit more so that I could see the whole thing.

It was a lot bigger than I expected.

A cold chill passed over me. The number I'd killed here in this building barely even dented their ranks. Hell, there were so much more on this list than I could have ever imagined.

I swallowed heavily and zoomed back in until I found Nicolai's name somewhere in the middle.

"Nicolai isn't particularly high on this family tree," I whispered cautiously.

"No. He isn't," Lawson replied.

"You knew that already?"

"Nicolai is the reigning face of the Venuti family, but I've always suspected that there would be someone behind him pulling the strings," he replied, searching the tree himself. "I recognize a great many names... Constantine, Barnabus, Demetri, among others."

Toboe rounded the desk and stood beside me. He plugged a USB drive into the computer tower and typed in a few keystrokes, initiating a full backup.

"I don't see us getting interrupted, but I think it would be useful to take all of this information to go," he offered.

"For sure," I echoed. I glanced down and pressed my thighs together, feeling myself flush with heat at the realization that he could see that I was still bare from the waist down. I shifted in my seat as the burn from Lawson's belt intensified for a second. I chewed my lip, feeling the residual soreness in my bottom hole too. To Toboe's credit, he didn't even glance down to look at me, but the knowledge that he could potentially see Lawson's seed drying on my thighs made me blush even deeper with shame.

I swallowed hard and tried to focus back on the screen.

I opened a few more folders, seeing nothing of interest until I stumbled across one that was simply named Winters. I double clicked on it as fast as I could. The first thing that popped up was an image of my father's face. For a moment, I just sat there and stared into the kindness in his eyes. I wished I could reach out and touch him.

I just wanted to tell him that I loved him, one last time.

The Venuti had taken that from me.

As if he could feel the tension inside me, Lawson pressed his palm firmly against my shoulder and squeezed it tight.

"Together," he whispered softly.

I reached up and took his fingers in mine, holding them tightly and I took that one last leap of faith. I decided to trust him in this.

"Together," I echoed, and he squeezed me tighter.

I opened the next picture and sucked in a shaky breath.

It was the two of us, together in a park.

I remembered that day like it was yesterday.

It was taken on my eighteenth birthday. I could still feel the cold chill of the mint chocolate chip ice cream running down my wrist, the crisp taste of the frosty treat on my tongue and the warm embrace of the sun on my face as it broke free of the clouds above us. The hustle and bustle of the quarter rushed all around us, the clopping of the horse-drawn carriages, the laughter of the tourists that were already drunk at noon on a Saturday, and the delicious scent of fried seafood swirling all around us, the beep of a car horn somewhere in the distance.

I could still hear my father's laugh as I rushed to eat that ice cream cone before it totally melted in my hands.

"You miss him," Lawson whispered gently.

"I do," I answered hoarsely.

"We're going to clear his name," he vowed, and his voice shook just the tiniest bit with emotion.

"Why would you want to help me? You've seen what he's done. You don't even know him," I said softly.

"I know it saddens you, sweet girl, and I want to take that away. I want to see you smile. I want to see you happy," he murmured. His fingers squeezed even tighter on my shoulder, and I knew he was speaking the truth. I didn't know what to say so I just tightened my fingers on his.

My heart faltered just a bit as he guided my hand back toward the mouse. He opened another file, and we began to read together.

As a team.

I took a shallow breath and scanned over the first document. It was just his resume, a summary of various projects that he'd worked on, his job history, everything he could list publicly at least. I clicked on another after that, and the real information started to come out.

There'd been a contract that had been written up between him and the vampires of the quarter.

And it had only been signed by one party. Nicolai Venuti.

Beneath a blank signature line, my father's full name had been typed out. I sat back and stared at it for a long time.

I scrolled back up and devoured the details of that document.

I'd known that the Venuti had wanted him to work with them, but I hadn't known the details as to what that was. At least, not until now.

They wanted him to create weapons for them. A lot of weapons.

They didn't want just guns or bombs or the usual things that would be used in the normal world. They had demanded that my father create weapons that could be used against the shifter families, things like silver-tipped bullets, a weaponized aeration of wolfsbane that could be used to take down an entire shifter pack, and so much more. They wanted weapons that were much higher tech than what was available now, easier to produce and stable in long-term storage. The more I read, the more uneasy I felt until I finished the whole thing and sat back. I licked my lips, reluctant to say anything for a long time.

Finally, I cleared my throat.

"The Venuti were preparing for war," I breathed as I turned toward Lawson. "They've been readying themselves for war against you."

I opened more files, finding blueprints of the silver-tipped bullets my father had already created and research articles that pointed to the aeration of the one plant that made shifters weak, wolfsbane. There were more that suggested potential research avenues that I could only assume would result in exposing a weakness in the wolves, but all of it had been gathered in preparation of my father's assumed cooperation.

There were letters demanding his compliance, including threatening notes of blackmail that were directed at his financial well-being and a few that even threatened my life.

He had refused. All of it.

Three days before the massacre, my father had come here and met with Nicolai. He hadn't left the building that day, nor had he left the day after. The morning of his release, my father had walked right into the French Quarter, what I now knew was shifter territory, and killed a number of tourists and locals in a bloody massacre that resulted in his death.

I opened the last file in the folder, which described the events of the day he'd come here all the way to the termination of my father's life at the hands of the Venuti men. It not only confirmed that the vampires had been the one to kill him, but it listed them all by name.

Lawson cleared his throat.

"You know of vampires, Ava, but do you know about the different abilities the vampire families have?" he asked softly.

"I'm not sure I know what you mean," I answered.

"Vampires are the natural predators of humankind, but the Venuti have had an easier time of that than many of the other clans. You see, when around humans they have an enhanced sort of charisma and I think your father knew that. He was taking a special herb that guarded against it, but there's a window of time here that it appears that the Venuti held him prisoner, which would be just enough time for that herb to work its way out of his system," Lawson explained.

"A special herb?"

"Have you ever heard of blackthorn, Ava?"

I shook my head.

"It safeguards humans against vampires, specifically of the Venuti Clan. In ancient Greece, humans would hang it above the gates to their house. It was said to keep away the undead, but if ingested, it also protects those from the power of the Venuti compulsion. It needs to be ingested consistently though. I think Nicolai knew that your father was taking it. He kept him here, probably as a prisoner in the very cells I freed you from, until the blackthorn passed out of his system. When that time came, I think Nicolai compelled your father to do what he did. The location of the shooting hadn't been a mistake. It had been a message for me, and I'd missed its meaning then, but I understand now," he continued.

"They were warning you that war was coming," I whispered.

"Your father refused them, so they punished him for it. They could have forced him to work for them using their ability over the human mind, but they didn't. They had already set their eyes on someone else to make weapons for them. I'm sure of it."

"And if that person refused too, they could show them what they did to my father," I spat.

"Exactly," he answered.

"The backup is complete, boss," Toboe murmured, and Lawson grunted in acknowledgement.

"We should get out of here," Lawson added. "That Venuti tree could come crashing down on us at any minute."

He offered me his hand and I took it. He led me around the desk, and I went to reach down for my discarded pants on the floor, but he stopped me.

"No. You're not going to be needing those," Lawson purred.

My pussy clenched tight just as my cheeks flared hot in embarrassment.

"But I—" I objected, and he shook his head. I glanced at Toboe and then back at Lawson. I chewed my lip and gasped lightly as he knelt before me and guided my feet back into my combat boots. When he was finished, he stood up and firmly grasped my upper arm. He led me out of Nicolai's office into his personal elevator. We rode it down to the ground floor and exited through the back of the building where there was a car already waiting for us. We didn't meet anyone on the way out, probably because I'd systematically killed everyone on my way inside.

I smiled a bit pridefully at myself, but it quickly passed as his fingers brushed against my bare cheeks, reminding me of the shameful things that had happened up there on the penthouse floor. I stared down at my feet and tried to focus on literally anything except how bare I was below my waist, which turned out to be impossible.

With every step, I was reminded of the welts he'd left behind with his belt, but that wasn't all. I could still feel the soreness of what he'd done to my bottom hole, and I whimpered anxiously just thinking about it. If he heard, he said nothing at all but the smirk on Toboe's face said everything. Lawson held open the car door and gestured for me to get in.

Blushing even more so, I rushed into the back seat, trying to use my hands to cover my pussy and my well-spanked bottom even if I knew it wouldn't do any good. I sat down quickly and used my hands to cover between my thighs. Lawson slipped into the back with me, while Toboe took the driver's seat.

Rather forcefully, he brushed my hands aside and replaced them with his own.

I tried to push him away, but he shook his head gently. I knew better than to keep pressing my luck, so I put my hands at my sides. He smiled victoriously.

"Open your legs. I want that bare little pussy on display for me," he coaxed. His words weren't threatening or demanding, but expectant and I found myself wanting to obey him. With a nervous swallow, I did as he asked and in reward, he slipped a finger in between my legs. His fingertip slid easily through my wet folds and brushed over top of my clit firmly enough to make me cry out with pleasure.

I was so very aware of every inch of my skin even though only my lower half was naked. If anything, still wearing a shirt was that much more shameful and made me so much more aware of the areas that were bare. I licked my lips and lifted my gaze, only to see his gaze level with mine.

"Little mate, you're still so very wet for me, aren't you?"

Almost impossibly, I blushed harder.

"Yes, alpha," I answered softly.

Was that okay? Was there something wrong with me for reacting like this?

The car drove away from the back of the Venuti tower and pulled back onto the street. I wanted to close my thighs for fear that someone might see me from the sidewalk, but I didn't. I held them open for him because I wanted to please him. He smiled as if he could read my thoughts, rewarding me with increasing pressure on my clit.

"What comes next?" I asked carefully and his grin widened. There was a sparkle in his gaze that both excited me and caused a nervous thrill to race down my spine. My core clenched tightly in anticipation, and I waited for him to answer me.

He brushed a stray lock of hair off my forehead, and I closed my eyes, enjoying the electricity that his touch elicited on my skin.

"You're so very beautiful when you're blushing and nervous for me, my pretty mate," he said softly, and I swear my face got even hotter.

His smile only got bigger.

His finger teased me, edging me with promise and something even more. I didn't think it would be possible, but he was pushing me back into a needy place once again.

"I'm going to take you back to my home, walk you through the front doors, and admire the marks my belt left behind on your bare little bottom. Then I'm going to lead you up to my bedroom and I'm going to claim you in the way an alpha should," he murmured.

Every muscle in my body tightened with anticipation.

"I left you behind last night and you escaped me, but I don't intend to allow you such privilege ever again. You're mine, and I intend to show you exactly what that means," he promised.

I fidgeted on the seat and that only served to rub my clit even more firmly against his fingers. I grinned knowingly and did it again. He didn't move to stop me, and I felt a tiny sliver of courage simmer up from deep inside me. I searched his face, all the while coaxing that boldness forth and when it was at its strongest, I pushed myself up from the seat and sat on his lap, one knee to either side of his hips. I centered myself so that my naked pussy was pressed up firmly against his cock. The only barrier between us was the fabric of his slacks.

"You can do whatever you like, little mate, but if you come without permission, I'm going to have to deal with you more firmly than I intended when we get home."

"What if I want that?" I asked, feeling salaciously naughty for even saying so.

The yellow in his irises grew brighter, the beast in him coming out just for me.

It felt so dirty to be on top of him like this. I knew that Toboe could look in the rearview mirror and see all of me, but for some reason that only made me burn even fiercer. I roped my arms around Lawson's neck and leaned forward, brushing my lips against his while I rubbed my clit against his cock. I rolled my hips, dragging myself along his length and I groaned, a fiery jolt of pleasure twisting through me from within.

"Naughty girl. Are you trying to get yourself off on my cock?" he whispered devilishly, and I smirked, unable to hold in an anxious giggle at the filthy words coming from his mouth.

"What of it?" I sassed and he chuckled dangerously.

I pressed my lips against his, kissing him tentatively at first before I started to grow bolder. I could feel his amusement in my taking the lead and I wondered how long he'd allow me to get away with it.

I dragged my teeth along his lower lip, before I bit it lightly but as hard as I dared. I wanted to test him, and his grin only widened.

"Such a defiant little thing," he murmured, but there was a perilous edge to his words that made me shudder with desire.

The car rolled to a stop, and I casually glanced out of the window to see that we were somewhere in the middle of the quarter. My thighs flexed against his waist, and I couldn't help but think about the fact that some of the people walking by might be able to see me like this.

It made me feel like a wild primal thing and that sent a zing of arousal straight down to my clit.

His fingers glided along the curve of my throat before they gripped my chin just hard enough to hurt. In that moment, he took possession of me with his mouth. His tongue danced with mine, owning me. Taking me. Claiming me and I breathed in a shaky sigh. The car started to move again.

So did my hips.

He pulled away from me, but his hand never left my throat. His fingers tightened just a little and a soft moan escaped me. There was no stopping it, even if I had wanted to.

"Even with your bottom welted and sore inside and out, you're such a brave little thing, aren't you?" he asked, his voice edged with darkness and my blush only deepened.

He was right.

I pushed harder, rocked my hips back and forth faster. I could feel my arousal building in my core and then the sound of his own groan of pleasure nearly pushed me over the edge. He chuckled and I gasped as his fingers squeezed my throat a bit harder.

"Are you trying to come, little mate?"

"Yes, alpha," I purred. I ground into him a bit harder.

"I didn't give you permission, did I?"

"No, alpha," I answered, chewing the bottom of my lip anxiously.

"What do you think will happen if you come without your alpha's permission, little mate?" he pressed, his eyes glinting dangerously and I stared back at him, standing at the precipice of defiance and obedience. I had to make a choice.

"You'll punish me, alpha," I murmured, feeling my inner core heat as the true meaning of those words washed over me.

"I will, sweet mate," he grinned. "When we reach my home, I'm going to take you to my bedroom and claim you in the way that you need to be claimed. The only thing up to you is whether that claiming will be gentle or rough."

I blushed harder.

"Do I make myself clear, little one?"

I stared down at his chest. I did know. With a hard swallow, I tried to decide on my next move. I studied his dark gaze, wavering back and forth before I realized something about myself.

Gentle didn't leave me shaking with pleasure. Gentle didn't make me quiver and needy for more.

I needed his roughness. I wanted the savage beast that I knew was inside him.

I rolled my hips again, a slight smirk playing at my lips. I was playing with fire, and I knew it, but I wanted to get burned.

Maybe he was right, and it was fate playing at my emotions, but it felt like maybe we were meant to be together. I hadn't known I was looking for a man like him. I'd felt it from the very first time I'd laid eyes on him, and he'd freed me from my prison cell. He'd known it too and he hadn't listened to my protest. He'd just taken me because he wanted me.

"Maybe I want to be a bad girl," I purred softly.

His eyes danced at my challenge.

"Your defiance is making my cock very, very hard, little mate," he snarled, his own need for me broaching on ravenous.

I could feel every inch of his thick length beneath me. He wasn't lying. He was really hard for me, and I liked that. My thighs squeezed around his waist, and I ground against him with more enthusiasm.

I pressed my lips to his cheek.

"You don't want me to make love to you gently, do you?"

"No, alpha," I answered, feeling light in my rebelliousness. It felt like I was floating on air and when I came down, I knew he would be there to catch me when I fell. I grinned.

The fall was going to be the most enjoyable part.

I clutched at his shoulders, and he made no move to stop me. His fingers slung around my throat, feeling like liquid fire until they clutched at the hair at the back of my scalp.

He pulled it. Hard.

I keened, pain blossoming across my head, radiating down my spine, and settling in the needy center between my thighs.

"If you come now, mate, it's going to hurt when I fuck this pretty little cunt as hard as I please. I promise you that," he purred.

"I'm counting on it," I growled ferociously, and he growled even more viciously.

"Oh, little one, I'm looking forward to it," he murmured with a seductive groan.

I started to move faster, feeling needier and even more aroused with every roll of my hips. His grip on my hair tightened, causing tendrils of pain and pleasure to rebound inside me with wild abandon. My eyes started to roll back in my head and my nipples pulsed, still safely encased within the cups of my bra. I rode him harder, the rough fabric of his slacks driving me closer to the edge of a pleasurable bliss I was going to take myself. Without permission.

The glimmer of danger in his eyes made it all the hotter.

With his other hand, he gripped my bottom cheek and squeezed the welts he'd put there. The painful sting was enough to force me to the very edge of that orgasm I sought.

"If you're going to come without permission, you better make sure that you scream while you do it. Make sure that

Toboe knows exactly what you're doing on your alpha's cock, my bad little girl," he purred.

I lost it after that.

My hips rocked back and forth at a furious pace. My eyes rolled back, and my fingers squeezed at his shoulders. In the back of my mind, I feared that I may be hurting him, but I realized that was silly. He was a wolf. I was a human.

He was the one who was going to hurt me, and I was going to like it.

I started to tremble on top of him, overwhelmed by the consuming pleasure coursing through me. The pain from his grip on the back on my head turned into a vicious sort of bliss and I couldn't get enough of it.

Oh, fuck.

It was hot disobeying him like this.

I couldn't wait to find out how he was going to punish me.

My orgasm raged on, sizzling through my body like wildfire. Untamed and feral. His cock was more than rock hard, and I rode it like I was made for it.

Maybe I was.

I screamed, throwing my head back as much as I could manage and lost myself on top of his cock. My pleasure poured over me, vicious and primal.

Our attraction had its softness and hard edges, a beautiful mix of rough beauty and heart.

I knew then that I was falling for him in a big way and from that point forward, there would be no going back.

I clutched at him as I took my stolen pleasure, enjoying every last moment of my rebelliousness knowing that he was going to punish me for it later.

"That's it, sweet mate. Let me hear you scream as you defy me," he purred.

I did. I worried that I screamed too loud, but as I shattered, I realized that I didn't much care. I shook on top of him, my clit throbbing with pleasure and my pussy tightening desperately against him. I wanted to feel him inside me.

Badly.

The car pulled to a stop and Lawson released the hair at the back of my head.

"We've reached my home, little mate. I will give you a moment to gather yourself. When you're ready, you will tell me, and I will walk you inside. I want you to think about how I'm going to use that sweet little cunt in just a little while and then I want you to think about how much it's going to hurt when I thrust into you tonight," he warned, and a shudder raced down my spine.

I don't know how he did it, but I already wanted to come for him again.

"Do you understand me, little mate?" he asked gently.

The blood was still racing underneath my skin, so I nodded at first before I remembered to answer in the way he expected.

"Yes, alpha," I purred.

"Good," he answered. "I'm looking forward to watching that bare little bottom walk inside my front door, but do you know what I'm looking forward to seeing even more?"

"No, alpha," I answered, blushing heartily at the disguised promise in his tone.

"I'm looking forward to seeing that wet little pussy peeking out from between those pretty thighs as you walk up the stairs to my bedroom," he whispered in my ear, just loud enough so that I could hear. A quiet sigh of shame fell of my lips and the only thing I could think to do was hide my face in the crook of his shoulder.

He pressed his lips against the side of my head and my heart fluttered inside my chest.

I hadn't even known I had been missing something like this until he'd found me.

I didn't know if I'd ever be able to let that go again. I did know that I didn't want to.

My heart pulsed and I grinned before I pushed off of him.

"Lead the way, wolf," I sassed and the growl that followed set my core on fire.

The quiet rumble of the engine cut off and I heard Toboe open the driver's side door behind me. It shut with a click, and I saw him walk around the car before he opened the door next to us. I went to climb off his lap, but Lawson shook his head. He held me there and I fidgeted against him, feeling exceptionally naughty to be sitting there on his cock with his beta watching.

"My mate is beautiful, isn't she, Toboe?" Lawson asked.

I cried out softly in shame, unable to hide the way my embarrassment catapulted out of my control. I hid my face once more, but he grasped my bottom firmly in his fingers as a firm reminder that he could do what he wanted, when he wanted with me.

"She is indeed, alpha," Toboe observed. I didn't even have to look to feel his eyes on me and it made me tremble a bit even as I was wrapped in Lawson's arms.

I chewed my lip anxiously as Lawson finally decided to lift me off his lap. He placed me down on the seat behind him and climbed out first. He stood outside the door and offered his hand for me to take. Feeling vulnerable in my arousal, I tentatively took his fingers within mine. My eyes flicked downward, and I hummed with shameful need at the hard line of his cock still safely encased in his slacks.

It was only when I noticed the wet spot that I'd left behind that I was forced to look away. My nipples tightened and my clit pulsed with need. I tried to ignore it as he pulled me out of the car, but it only grew stronger now that I was outside the safety of the car. It felt so wrong to have my pussy and bottom bare while I was standing outside. Nervously, I looked around and tried to see if there was anyone else out there. The property seemed pretty private and off the beaten path. On the border was a high fence, with a thick towering wall of vegetation in front of it. From what I could tell, it was just the three of us out here in the night.

My gaze passed slowly around the perimeter until it settled on the massive mansion set at the center of the property.

"Are we still in the quarter?" I sighed in wonder and my alpha wound his arm around my shoulders, pulling me tight against him.

"We're a little bit outside of it, but still close enough so that we can watch over it from the top floor," he explained.

To say the house was gigantic would have been an understatement, but it was still so beautifully done. It was built in the style of a southern plantation. The bright lights hidden within the gorgeous flowerbeds cast the house in shadow and glowing light that was the same color as the full moon. It was at least five stories tall, and the front porch was lined with thick wooden pillars that shone bright even in the darkness of night. It was grand and beautiful and as I studied the picturesque home, it felt perfectly suited to the man holding me against him.

"Welcome to Crescent Manor, little mate. Tomorrow, I'll give you a full tour and introduce you to several members of my pack, but not tonight. Tonight, I'm going to take care of you," he purred, and I hummed with excitement. His head turned toward Toboe, and I felt him nod. I watched as Lawson's beta walked toward the house. He entered the home and left the door ajar. Casually, he turned back to gaze at the two of us before he strode inside, leaving us alone.

The tension between Lawson and me was heavy. I could feel it pulsing between us and my lungs screamed for oxygen as though I was deep under water and couldn't make it to the surface in time to draw in a breath.

His touch glided along my collarbone, pushing just beneath my shirt to scorch my skin. My heart pounded in my chest, and I knew there would be no getting it under control again. He felt scary and dangerous, but at the same time, he felt safe, and I wanted his hands on all of me once again.

His hand fell away from my body slowly, almost reluctantly and my heart drummed even faster knowing that things were about to escalate.

My core pulsed with heat.

"You're going to walk into my home in a moment and I'm going to follow you. As you take each step for me, I want you to think about how you defied me in the car, how you took your own pleasure without permission, and how you ignored my warning that you would pay for that indulgence when I took you up to my bedroom tonight. I want you to think about how that time is now. When we go upstairs, I want you to imagine what it's going to be like when I decide to take my own pleasure from every inch of this beautiful, defiant little body," he murmured, and I gasped audibly in needy shock at the filthiness in his instructions. For several long moments, I just wavered on my feet, feeling lost in my own neediness and open desire.

"Do you understand me, little mate?" he asked.

"Yes, alpha," I answered, my voice far too shaky.

"Walk for me now, mate, and remember that I'm very much enjoying the sight of your bare, welted little bottom swaying back and forth," he ordered, and I tried to temper the smile that graced my lips, but it broke free anyway.

I took that first step and my legs felt like jelly, but I held my head high and then I pushed forward with another. My chest rose and fell with the heavy knowledge that he was watching my every move and that he was enjoying that sight.

I whimpered quietly at the thought that it was probably making his cock hard too.

I climbed the few stairs that led up to the porch and walked across it, glancing nervously over my shoulder to see him following me with a hungry seductive expression painted on his face. I lost my nerve just as quickly and looked away, making myself focus on the floor in front of me as I crossed the threshold of his home. Once inside, I paused and admired the massive metal chandelier above my head.

Wooden beams crisscrossed above my head, immense and spectacular against solid white ceilings. To either side of me was a sweeping staircase made of hard wood with beautiful wrought-iron handrails curving up to a high balcony that appeared to have hallways going off to the left and right.

Nothing was overstated, but it was extraordinarily elegant all the same. It all came together with a sense of beautiful perfection that took my breath away.

"Do you like it?" he asked softly as he approached me from behind.

"I adore everything about it," I whispered.

"I'm glad because this is now your home too," he said firmly and even in its forcefulness, it made me smile.

"It's beautiful," I beamed, and his arm lightly pressed against my lower back, guiding me toward the right side of the staircase. I remembered myself and took another shaky step, feeling my thighs slide against one another. I lifted my foot and climbed the first stair, followed by the second and I noticed that he had stopped to watch me.

"Keep going, sweet mate," he coaxed, and I took several more steps slowly, more than aware of how much this little interlude was turning me on. Once I'd climbed the stairs about halfway, he growled, and I could have sworn that it was the hottest thing I'd ever heard in my life.

"Your arousal is glistening on those pretty thighs, mate. You're wet for me," he observed, and a soft whine flew free from my lips. By the time I reached the second floor, I was absolutely drenched.

I turned to face him, and he started to climb the stairs too, taking each step carefully and steadily, prolonging the time we were apart and making everything inside me burn up with scorching need. I watched him come for me and for a second, I considered running but that wasn't an option any longer. I lifted my chin, coaxing my bravery forth and fidgeted anxiously as I waited for him to take me.

He took my hand in his grasp and led me off down the hallway and I was too far gone with my own desire to pay much attention to what it looked like until we reached a tall wooden door at the end of it. He opened it as if he owned the place, which he probably did, and he led me inside. He led me forward just enough so that he could shut the door behind me. I heard the lock click and I knew there was no stopping what was to come.

Not that I wanted to...

I'm not sure where it had happened, but there was a shift between us. The element of his heavy-handedness had been difficult at first, and I'd fought him tooth and nail, but now I saw it for what it was. He wanted to claim me as his, his possessiveness so thorough that he'd just taken me knowing that I would come to see that as something I adored about him.

His finger slid over my hipbone, slow and steady. I sighed, just feeling the way his simple touch elicited waves of electricity to course through me. He knelt down beside me and removed my boots and socks, leaving me all too aware of the face that his cheek was resting against my skin as he did so. I took in one shaky breath after another, trying to keep myself still. I wanted to touch him. I needed to touch him.

I resisted because I wanted to enjoy this part too.

He stood back up and slipped his fingers beneath the hem of my shirt, lifting it up over my head shortly thereafter. With a single quick snap, he undid the clasp of my bra and that fell away too, leaving me completely bare and vulnerable before him.

Oh, God.

I pressed my thighs together. I wasn't sure why but there was a part of me that wanted to hide my body even though he'd already seen it. I didn't know what to do with my hands, so I folded them behind my back as he walked around me and gazed into my eyes. I saw everything in his stare, the dark promises of what he was going to do to me tonight and tomorrow and the night after that.

I'd never felt so aroused in my life.

He looked at me like I was the most beautiful thing in the world and that made my heart leap with joy.

"You're perfect, my pretty little mate," he breathed, and I blushed, unsure what to do with his unexpected praise. He took a step toward me and lifted my chin, capturing my lips in a soft kiss before he drew away.

I breathed in his scent, trembling and wanting and entirely too needy.

"And now I'm going to show you what it means to be mine," he murmured, and I cried out in fear and desire too powerful to contain.

His gentleness had run out.

He slid his hands down to my backside and lifted me straight off the floor, his fingers gripping at my sore bottom roughly.

He turned and tossed me on his bed, looking down at me like the savage beast I knew him to be.

"Spread your legs, mate. Show me that needy little pussy," he demanded and with a touch of fearful hesitation, I did just as he asked.

His eyes dropped to study me, and I drew my lower lip into my mouth nervously. The salacious grin that graced his mouth made me want to hide once more, but I kept my legs open because that was what he wanted. All of his focus was on me right now and it made me feel wanted in such a beautiful way that I couldn't get enough of it.

I wanted more.

He approached the bed, never taking his eyes from the wetness between my thighs. With a steady sureness, he reached for me and traced his thumb through the arousal that had dripped down onto my inner thigh.

"Do you feel this, mate? Do you see how your body recognizes your alpha?" he purred.

"Yes, alpha," I breathed heatedly, trying to study his gaze for some hint of what he wanted and finding nothing but the mask that was him. The unknown burned me up inside and I couldn't stop myself from arching my body toward him.

I felt like I was sizzling up from within.

Then he started unbuttoning his shirt. There was no way I could look away as his strong fingers undid each button one at a time, slowly revealing the cotton undershirt he was wearing underneath. Finally, he shrugged off both shirts, leaving me to revel in the hard lines of his chest. He kicked off his shoes and his hands dropped to his belt.

I gulped, remembering how that very thing had punished me hard enough to leave its mark on my naked backside.

He undid his pants and pushed them down his hips, revealing his cock with a certain swiftness that left me breathless. My heart pounded and time seemed to slow as I took in his thick length. I reveled in the sight of it.

His cock was hard for me.

And in just a little while, I was going to have in deep inside me.

He climbed onto the bed and over top of me and I was more than aware of his thick length as it brushed against the sensitive skin of my thighs. I sucked in an anxious breath as its vivid heat took its rightful place between my thighs. He didn't enter me just yet, but the insinuation was there. I knew he'd thrust into me very soon and I also knew it was going to hurt. It was going to make me come all the harder for that reason.

He kissed me ruthlessly hard, taking me with forceful savagery and I returned his kiss with just as much enthusiasm.

"You're mine, mate. From now on, every sigh of pleasure, every scream, every last gasp of need is mine to give. I'm going to keep all of it for myself, do you understand me?" he snarled. His breath tickled my ear and I shivered in his arms.

"Show me," I pushed, and I could feel him grinning against my ear.

His fingers grazed along my neck and slipped underneath my scalp. I stared up into his eyes as he gripped my hair roughly enough so that a stinging pain radiated sharply across it. I gasped as it spread across the back of my head, shooting down to send a terrible insistent pulse directly to my clit. My pussy clamped down tightly in expectation, but I waited.

I waited for him to take control.

"When you rode my cock in the car, little mate, I realized something. Do you know what that was?"

"No, alpha," I whispered, trying to grapple with the overwhelming shame and unfathomable arousal that his words stoked inside me.

"I realized that I very much enjoyed seeing you come for me. I've decided that I'm going to enjoy that a whole lot more tonight," he vowed, and my hips surged up toward his in open need.

"You're a greedy little thing, aren't you?" he asked and I pressed myself up toward him.

I didn't know if I could survive much more of his teasing.

My body was jittery with arousal, and it took everything in me not to grind myself up and down the velvet softness of his thick length between my thighs.

"Punish me, alpha. Punish your mate," I pushed as bravely as I could. His eyes sparkled with darkness as he lined the head of his cock up to my entrance.

"I'm going to take you, my naughty little mate. You will wait until I give you permission to come for me. If you defy me this time, I will spank that pretty little cunt bright red and put you to bed wet and needy," he growled.

I squeaked nervously.

"Yes, alpha," I whispered.

He didn't give me a chance to say anything more because his hips jerked forward and the full length of his cock speared into me with one painful thrust.

I screamed and his lips descended onto mine.

He didn't start slow or gentle, nor did I expect him to. He'd promised me rough, and he delivered. Once he was fully inside me, he didn't pull out. Instead, he stayed there, enjoying the way my pussy struggled to take his massive size. My inner walls clutched at him, burning and fluttering with pain and pleasure far too intense to ignore.

It was everything.

"Tonight, I'm going to teach you how an alpha fucks his mate," he growled, and my legs squeezed tight at his hips.

"Oh, please," I begged.

He chuckled and slammed into me hard.

My fucking began rough and fast. It hurt from the very start, but I'd known it would. I wrapped my arms around him, clutching at his back and holding on for what I knew was going to be a night to remember. His cock surged in and out of me with ruthless intention, claiming me like I imagined a beast would. Really, though, he *was* a beast.

He was *my* beast.

His pelvis ground firmly against my clit with every thrust and I lost myself in the sensation of his cock slamming in and out of me, of the pleasure burning inside my core and the knowledge that a powerful orgasm was coming whether I wanted it or not.

I wanted it all. I needed it all and he was going to give it to me.

"I like the feel of your body struggling to take my cock. It makes me even harder," he growled.

"Oh!" I cried out and his fingers slipped down the front of my chest to capture my nipple in a painful twist. My pussy tightened around him, and the most delicious groan fell off his lips and reverberated all around me.

His cock was so hard, and it throbbed inside me, stretching me beautifully beneath him as he took what he wanted and, in that moment, I gave him everything.

The relationship between us wasn't soft, and I knew it would never be. It had claws that left me covered in his mark, teeth that had already sunk deep into my heart, and a bond that had begun to settle in the darkest depths of my soul.

My hips began to rock in tune with his, taking him deeper with every thrust. When I woke tomorrow, I knew that even my cervix would be sore.

I liked that.

My core sizzled and squeezed in tight, pleasure and pain coming together in a delicious mixture of perfection that consumed me. I suffered in the beautiful embrace of both sensations, enjoying every moment as my clit pulsed greedily against him.

It wouldn't be long before I shattered beneath him.

"Please. I need you," I whispered.

"I know, sweet girl. You will be patient for me. If you come before I say, you're not going to come again tonight," he warned, and I tried to remember to be obedient. My pleasure magnified, swirling inside me like a storm, growing stronger with every passing second and the only thing that kept it at bay was my need to please him.

My fucking grew rougher and faster and soon enough, I was so desperate that I began to beg. Even though I was so focused on obeying his instruction, I was fearful that I wouldn't be able to follow it for very much longer.

He punished me harder with his cock.

"I'm enjoying this greedy little pussy, my little mate," he snarled.

"Please. I need to come, alpha," I pleaded.

"You're going to have to be more convincing than that," he taunted, and I could feel his chuckle of amusement at my distress.

My clit pulsed, hot and heavy. Painful need billowed out inside me, and I felt as if I was floating on air. I could feel myself beginning to fall and I tried to keep myself from giving into the raging need that was surging through my veins, but it was so very hard.

"Alpha!" I screamed. "Please let me come for you. Please. Please."

"Do you think you deserve to come for me?" he asked, slowing his thrust to a leisurely pace that drew out my pleasure even further.

I met his gaze, searching his eyes with mine, pleading for him to grant me mercy. The way his cock slid in and out of me was a sinful torture. I wanted to come so badly that I felt like I could cry if he didn't allow it.

"Please," I begged.

"Answer the question, little mate," he growled, accentuating each syllable with a forceful thrust. I gasped with each one.

I didn't know the correct answer. I tried to read what he wanted from the steady firmness in his gaze, but I couldn't figure out what he expected me to say.

I tried to find my voice and it came out in something of a fractured whine.

He punished me with his cock then and I writhed beneath him. I cried. I begged.

"Please! Yes, alpha! Yes, I deserve to come for you!" I shrieked. My voice came out broken and weak, but I said the words anyway because he wanted to hear them.

"I think you deserve to come for me too, my sweet mate. I think you deserve to come for me more than once tonight, don't you agree?"

I blushed hard because he was right.

"Yes, alpha," I whined. "Please."

His grip tightened on the back of my head.

"Good. Now come for me, mate. Don't you stop until I give you permission to stop," he purred. His words acted as if they were a direct conduit to my core and I snapped as his cock slammed into me all the way to the hilt.

That first orgasm poured over me like a summer rain, hot and wet and so sudden that I wasn't ready for it even though I'd wanted it so badly. His body surrounded mine like a dominant prison and I writhed within its confines. His body was strong and even in his roughness, I knew I was safe with him.

My inner walls gripped him tight, and I drowned in the harsh chasm of the pleasurable pain that wrecked me from within. My core squeezed down so hard that I began to panic, but his grasp on me only held me more firmly.

His gaze held mine and I tried to turn my head, but he growled in warning.

"No. I want to see the look in your eyes when you come for me on my cock," he demanded.

I cried out, overwhelmed by my orgasm and feeling myself beginning to fall into that familiar but terrifying void that I knew was coming. I knew he was going to demand a whole lot from me tonight.

"Shh. Focus on me. I've got you, little mate," he crooned, and his fingers grasped my chin hard enough to force me to do exactly as he wished. My inner walls convulsed around him, and I stared into the yellow depths of his irises.

His beast was coming out for me. I could see it.

I came harder because of it.

The yellow in his irises exploded into a bright gold that was as hypnotizing as it was beautiful. My thighs began to quiver, and I could feel that second release bridging closer and closer with every beat of my heart. My legs quaked faster, my blood surged in my veins, and I arched into him.

My nipples scraped against his chest.

I started to scream.

That second orgasm followed far too quickly after the first and the pain that came with it twisted me open. His cock savaged me from within and I broke into a million different pieces, tiny shards of glass that fell to the floor and shattered once more.

My eyes rolled back in my head, and he pulled me against him, offering the safety of his embrace as he ravaged me. The wet sounds of his cock sliding in and out of me were so shockingly noisy that I felt as if it surrounded me.

This wasn't gentle or kind or even remotely sweet.

It was filthy and wrong and so incredibly dirty that just thinking about it tomorrow was going to make me blush and stammer through my shame.

It was perfect.

It was us.

I clutched at him, my fingers digging into his back, and he didn't complain. He groaned and I whimpered, caught in the painful aching riptide of my orgasm beneath him.

"That's it, mate. Come for me," he demanded and just when my release reached a harrowing peak, the base of his cock started to inflate inside me. I began to panic, but his lips brushed against mine and that fear fell away.

"Trust in me, my pretty mate. You can take my knot. You're made for this," he purred.

"Yes, alpha," I breathed fearfully, but I trusted those words.

My body writhed with agony and ecstasy and just when I thought it was going to fade away, a third and final orgasm wrenched through me before I could prevent it.

He thrust his cock all the way inside me just as the base billowed out wide, stretching me so far open and making me scream. I could feel it hooking behind my pelvis, anchoring us together as one. His thick length throbbed hard inside me and when the first blazing hot spurt of his seed marked my insides, I came harder than I ever have before. His eyes went wild with feral need, and he leaned forward and bit the cusp of my shoulder.

His teeth tore into my flesh, holding me still as he forced me to take his bite, his knot, and his seed at the same time.

"Please!" I begged.

The pain from his bite faded into nothing and the only thing left was the sore ache from his cock. A blissful warmth blossomed across my shoulder, and I gasped at its magnificence. It spread outward and settled in the core of my heart, pulsing once, twice.

Forever.

For him.

His seed continued to spurt deep inside me. His knot held us together physically, but the bond between us exploded from his mark. It simmered with a mystical energy, a powerful magic that bonded us together forever as one.

It felt as if it was fate.

Like he'd been meant to find me in that prison cell. In my home. And in the Venuti tower.

"I don't want to love you," I whispered, my voice shaky and unsure and entirely too vulnerable, but I said it anyway because I needed to.

"In the end, it won't be up to you, my defiant little mate," he murmured just as the last vestiges of his seed lashed hot against my cervix.

His knot didn't deflate right away. Instead, it held us together and I found that I adored its aftermath. His body was hot against mine, chasing away the ceaseless trembling that quaked through me as I came down from that last orgasm. His arms surrounded me, and he pulled me to him as he lay down beside me.

"You're mine, Ava," he continued. "You bear my mark now as my mate. I will only ever have eyes for you."

I hid my face in his chest, feeling my pussy grasp his cock just as my heart beat strong for him, only for him. I smiled against him.

Who was I to fight fate?

CHAPTER 7

Lawson

The power of the bond simmered inside me. I'd known she was my mate since I'd first laid my eyes on her and now that she was mine, I felt like I could breathe for the very first time. There would never be anyone more important than her, nothing more precious than her life. All the evidence pointed that the Venuti were on the cusp of instigating a war, but that didn't really matter right now. It would be dangerous, but I had my mate by my side and that would make me stronger than I had ever been.

Her eyelashes fluttered on my chest, and I pulled her closer to me, wanting to feel all of her against me. My knot still held us locked together and when it finally began to deflate, the tiniest moan of disappointment escaped her lips and tickled the surface of my skin. When it was time, I pulled out of her, but I didn't let her go.

I was never going to forget the way her delightful little body had grasped tight around my cock. She'd gripped me so tight that I wasn't sure if she was trying to pull me in deeper or squeeze all of me right out. I closed my eyes, breathing in the sweet flowery scent of her hair. She'd wanted me at the same time she didn't, but I hadn't given her a choice. She came even harder for me for that reason alone.

She was perfect.

I could feel her blinking, and a slight tremor raced across her skin. I held her close and pressed my lips against the top of her head. Her trembling ceased for a few long seconds before it began again.

She needed me and I was going to take care of her.

Without preamble, I wound my arms around her and lifted her from the bed. She made a sound, something that was a mix of a gasp and a sigh, but I didn't say anything. Right now, I was making the decisions for her, and she was just going to have to accept that. I carried her into the massive master bath attached to my bedroom and sat on the ledge of the oversized jetted tub. I started the water and made sure that it was just the right temperature before I lowered her into it. Her cheeks pinkened beautifully as she pulled her knees into her chest. She folded her hands together and watched me with cautious curiosity as I poured a few fragrant oils into the water for her.

Once the tub had filled enough, I shut off the water and reached for her. Tentatively, she placed her fingers in mine and I situated her so that I could wash her hair. I poured a generous amount of shampoo into my palm and massaged it into her hair. My hands were gentle and the tension I'd noticed before gradually faded away until she was like putty in my hands.

When I was done washing her beautiful locks, I leaned her head back just enough to rinse it out while ensuring none of it got into her eyes. I moved onto conditioning her hair next, bathing her in silence. There was a certain subdued satiety to her, and I smiled. It was incredibly rewarding to know that I'd been the one to satisfy her so thoroughly.

I massaged her scalp and she moaned openly. A hard jolt of pleasure raced straight down to my cock. I was hard again. With a grunt, I ignored my own desire to take her again. She needed my gentleness now and then she needed to be put to bed.

I squeezed my hands around her upper arms, noting that the occasional aftershock was still making her muscles quiver. Not allowing myself to take my eyes off her for even a moment, I soaped up a small washcloth and began to smooth it over her body.

"What happens now?" she asked. There was no challenge in her voice, just simple curiosity and the slightest edge of acceptance.

"You stay here with me. This is going to be your home now. I will send my men to gather your things and they will bring whatever you need," I began. I didn't leave any room for argument, but I could tell she wasn't going to fight me based on the way her body sagged against the tub. I rubbed the washcloth up and down her arms, soaping her up slowly and she nodded quietly.

"Okay," she answered.

Her body stopped trembling and the bond squeezed tight between us, an invisible rope that tied us together forever as one. She reached for my hand, entwining my fingers within hers and I gripped them firmly. She sighed quietly and relaxed, releasing me once she was ready.

For a while longer, she let me finish bathing her in silence. I had her stand up for me so that I could wash the rest of her body. She blushed particularly hard when I glided the washcloth between her thighs, washing the remains of her own arousal and my seed from her skin. She whined softly when I reached around her waist and cleansed between her cheeks. Wanting to deepen her shame just a little more, I gently turned her around, inspecting the still pink marks on her pretty little bottom. I traced my fingers across a few of the darkest, noting that none of them would likely be there when she woke in the morning.

I took my hands and spread her cheeks wide open, and she cried out more in shock than anything else. I quietly studied her beauty.

"This little bottom hole is still pink, my pretty mate. Is it still sore from my cock?" I asked quietly.

"Yes, alpha," she squeaked, and I soaped up a single finger. When I pressed it against her sore hole, she clenched tight and tried to keep me out. I chuckled. She wouldn't.

I pushed hard enough to breach that tight hole and she moaned, the sound an intoxicating mix of pain and pleasure that made my cock even harder. Roughly, I pumped my finger in and out of her.

"I have to make sure you're clean, don't I, pretty mate?"

"Oh! Yes, alpha," she groaned, and I slipped another finger forward into her pussy, enjoying the feel of both of her pretty holes tightening around me.

If I wasn't careful, I wasn't going to be able to stop myself from fucking her once more.

I slipped my fingers out of her. She needed rest. There would be plenty of time for me to take her in the way she needed to be taken in the days to come.

I used another washcloth to rinse her off and when I was finished, I wrapped a warm fluffy towel around her. Without preamble, I lifted her from the tub and sat her on the ledge. I rubbed a light conditioner into the ends of her hair and combed it, taking extra care not to hurt her in the process.

Her eyelids grew heavy, and it soon became clear to me that she was having difficulty keeping them open. I quickly dried her off and lifted her once more, carrying her back into the bedroom. Much to her embarrassment, I unwrapped the towel and allowed my gaze to lazily study her naked form before I tucked her into bed.

I glided my thumb along her cheek and enjoyed the bond pulsing between us. She looked up at me through hooded eyes and I smiled down at her.

"Such a good girl," I whispered, and she beamed back at me with such happiness that it made my heart pulse just as joyfully in return.

"That was pretty intense," she murmured, and that pulse only grew stronger.

"Sleep now. I have some work to do before I come join you," I answered, unable to hide the giddy grin that was plastered all over my face now.

"Yes, alpha," she sighed, and I stayed just a little longer until I was certain that she was asleep.

She looked like an angel, but I knew that she was going to be a handful and I liked that. I was certain she was going to keep me on my toes. I was going to enjoy reminding her of her place beside me, over and over again until she screamed my name.

In fact, I was looking forward to it.

* * *

With much reluctance, I eventually convinced myself to leave the room. I returned to my office only to find Toboe hard at work inside it. I leaned against the door and feigned annoyance, clearing my throat so that he'd notice me. He lifted his head and smirked.

"What's up, boss?" he asked lightly.

"You're sitting at my desk," I replied, and his grin widened.

"I figured you wouldn't need it tonight," he answered, and I chuckled. "What? Did she wear you out already?"

"More like I gave her more than she could handle," I answered.

"Cocky bastard," he teased. "So did you make it official?"

"She bears my mark now, yes," I replied.

"Good. Good. I'm glad that's settled," he smirked. "Now, maybe we can talk about what else I found on Nicolai's computer before you want to head to bed yourself."

I strode forward and took a seat in the chair in front of my desk with a heavy sigh.

"It's worse than I think it is, isn't it?"

I could stop myself from rubbing the bridge of my nose in annoyance.

"There's been a lot of underhanded moves made by the Venuti that we haven't recognized. They've turned a few of our allies against us, taken over a few of the key businesses in the quarter, and made some sort of deal with the police to overlook their kills and hide them from us."

"Give it to me straight, Toboe," I grumbled.

"They've been preparing to stand against us for a long time and it appears that they are almost ready."

"Can you give me any sort of timeline?"

"Maybe a week. Or a month. Maybe more or maybe less. It's hard to gauge," he mused.

"Let's start with Ava's father then. I don't understand why they'd let him refuse them in the first place. Why not just make him do their bidding by force?"

"He wasn't the only one under contract with the Venuti to develop those weapons. They had another engineer on the line too, only he was far more cooperative than her father had been. There were multiple reasons they dealt with him as they did," he explained.

I narrowed my eyes.

"The first thing they wanted to do was test our ability to keep carnage out of the quarter. We failed on that one. Second, they wanted to send us a message, but we hadn't been looking for it and missed it. Third, the café was packed with tourists and locals alike, but the Venuti were only concerned with one particular woman who happened to be having coffee with her fiancé that day."

He paused dramatically and it annoyed me. He winked in my direction, knowing that it did.

"The governor's daughter," he added, and I sucked in a breath.

"Did she get shot that day?" I asked anxiously.

"She did."

"Did she die?"

"She did. At least according to the human records," he answered. He looked away from me and turned the computer monitor toward me.

It was the Venuti family tree. He zoomed in on the bottom and sat back in the chair, waiting for me to figure out what he hadn't yet said.

Lola Claiborne.

"They turned her," I sighed.

"Yeah. So, we can probably kiss our arrangement with the governor goodbye," Toboe replied, his voice carrying just as much frustration as I felt.

"Fuck me," I groaned.

"No. That's your mate's job," he replied, and it was so unexpected that I snorted with a laugh.

"You're not wrong," I smirked.

"I know," he answered.

"I take it there's more," I finally pressed.

"You'd be right. The engineer they employed instead of Ava's father had been slower to produce what they want, but he's been on the right track. So far, he's developed the silver-tipped bullets that they wanted, and they just so happen to be far easier to produce in mass quantities. It's only been in production for a month or so, but we need to be far more cautious in our dealings with them from now on," he continued.

"Fuck me twice," I sighed.

"No means no, boss," he smirked and once again, I shook my head, but I couldn't stop myself from smiling. His sarcasm was keeping my anger at the Venuti at bay, and I deeply appreciated that. I wasn't about to tell him though. It would most certainly go to his head.

I just laughed softly at him, and he chuckled.

"What you do to your mate on your time is none of my business," he murmured, and I laughed harder once I realized that he'd blushed just a little when he'd said that.

"So. Moving on. They wanted some sort of weapon laced with wolfsbane, but that hasn't really made much progress yet. Turns out the component that's actually effective against shifters is not particularly stable long term. Which is good for us."

"Indeed."

He started to list off a few more things and I listened attentively, sighing as I realized just how long this had been going on under my nose. They'd seemingly begun edging into the quarter for months, if not years now and they'd done it without any of my men noticing.

That was going to have to be dealt with. This was my territory and when the time came, I was going to show them that.

"They've been watching this property, boss. They'll know that we brought her here," Toboe continued, and I growled openly at the threat thrown her way even though it wasn't from him.

He was right. There was no way what she'd done tonight wouldn't be noticed.

"Do they have a file on her?" I asked.

He nodded.

"Tell me everything," I pressed.

"It's a rather basic profile. Name. Background. Job history. The usual things you might expect. It really didn't have much to it until this week when she made her first appearance inside their property. It does make a note of the type of bullets she was using. They know that she has something that could be highly dangerous if used against them in the future," Toboe replied. His voice was far graver now. He knew that this was probably the most dangerous part of what he's told me tonight.

"They're going to come for her," I said quietly.

"That may make them move faster than they intended," he replied.

"If they have enough bullets, it may make them overconfident," I replied thoughtfully.

"Maybe," he answered cautiously.

"Well, starting tomorrow, we're going to have to start preparing to welcome them with as much southern hospitality as they have come to expect," I replied firmly, and he laughed.

"That sounds like fun," he smirked.

"Oh, it will be. Now go to bed. We're going to need to get some sleep because things could start to get really interesting come morning," I added.

"Got it, boss."

"Night, Toboe. Thanks for having my back today."

"It was an honor," he grinned.

With a final nod, I pushed myself up and out of the chair. Toboe continued to work on the computer behind me as I walked out of the office. I didn't pay him any more mind because my mind had already turned back to the delightful little package curled up in my bed. I strode down the hallway and silently returned to my room. I stripped down to my underwear, and when I glanced down at her I noticed that her eyes had opened, and she was watching me sleepily with a wistful smile on her lips.

When she noticed that I had seen her, she turned her head and hid her face in the pillow. I'd seen her mouth curve up in an even bigger smile though. I rounded the bed and climbed into it with her, unapologetically winding my arm around her waist so that I could pull her flush against my chest.

"Did you miss me?" I whispered in her ear.

"No," she answered feistily.

I chuckled in her ear, and she shivered against me. Boldly, I dragged my fingers down the length of her abdomen and forced them in between her thighs.

She was very, very wet.

"Little mate, I think you're lying to me," I whispered. "I think you did miss me, and this pretty pussy is giving you up."

She trembled a bit harder.

I slid the tip of my finger over her clit, earning the most delicious moan of reluctant desire from her. I was holding her close enough against me so that she could feel just how hard she was making me.

"Alpha," she whimpered.

I teased her for a bit longer, enjoying every whimper that fell off her lips until I finally pulled my hand away, only to hear her sigh softly in disappointment.

"It is time for you to close your eyes, sweet girl. Tonight, you're going to go to bed wet and needy for me and tomorrow, I promise you I will take care of that greedy little pussy. Be a good girl for me and I might even make sure you enjoy it," I whispered in her ear.

She panted and it took everything in me not to sink every inch of me into her slick little cunt. I pressed my lips to the back of her head, kissing her softly.

She snuggled in a bit closer to me.

"Promise?" she whined.

"I promise, sweet mate. Now close your eyes. If you make me tell you again, I'll have to turn that bare little bottom bright red. Do you understand me?"

"Yes, alpha," she answered. Her fingers wrapped around mine and I squeezed them tight.

"Good girl," I murmured, placing a light kiss on the back of her neck. Her body softened at my praise, and I decided I'd have to give her more of that.

At least, when she earned it…

I closed my eyes too, content that I'd found the woman I was meant to cherish for the rest of my life.

Both with and without a red little bottom.

CHAPTER 8

Ava

When I woke the next morning, I knew that my whole life had changed, and I wasn't sure if it was for the better or for worse. Not only had I slept in a man's bed for the first time, but the gentle ache on my shoulder told me that something far deeper had occurred. I'd heard of wolf shifters and humans pairing together, but I hadn't believed it and I certainly never thought that it would happen to me. I was feeling the bond, the ever-pulsing energy that tied me to another through some sort of magical thread, a connection that bound me to him.

I took a deep breath, trying to keep myself still as I took stock of my limbs and the ceaseless pounding of my heart. There was almost a mystical energy to its constant drum in my chest, almost as if his and mine were beating as one. I didn't want to move for fear of waking him up, but when his chin brushed against my shoulder, I knew that he was already awake.

"How did you sleep?" he purred.

The mark throbbed and so did the infuriatingly needy clit between my thighs.

When had his voice turned into such pure liquid sex?

"Well," I answered, but my voice revealed just how aroused that simple question had made me.

He openly sniffed the air, and I couldn't help myself as I pressed my legs together, hoping that I would be able to hide what I inevitably already knew was there.

"I'm glad," he answered, and his fingers slipped between my thighs. "Just as wet as I left you," he murmured, and I couldn't stop the way my body responded to him with open invitation. My thighs parted of their own accord as his finger slid along my pussy. I gasped as fiery tendrils of pleasure raced up and down my legs.

Why was he so fucking good at that? Why did a single touch of his hand make me want to fall apart all over it?

"Lawson," I whined.

"Hmmm. Would you like to come for me, little mate?" he whispered hoarsely, the gravelly tone of his voice brushing against the tiny hairs on my ear and driving me wild with need.

With him, I was insatiable.

"Yes. Please, alpha," I answered excitedly, and his finger began to move faster and harder.

Fuck. He was going to make me come. Fast.

I don't know how he managed it, but I was on the precipice of orgasm within seconds. I could feel it building inside of me, a tiny little ball of desire that was quickly beginning to spiral out of control.

"You will wait until I give you permission, mate. I'm only going to allow you to have one orgasm this morning, so make sure you come very long and very hard for me."

His instruction only made holding on that much more difficult. My thighs began to shake at the effort it took to keep my orgasm at bay.

"If you fail to follow my instructions, I will spank that naughty little clit bright red and bring you downstairs wet, incredibly needy, and very sore."

I squirmed, trying to avoid his skillful fingers, but it didn't do much good. His arm held me captive around my waist as his touch danced on top of my clit, ceaseless and wonderful in the same breath.

"That's not all, sweet mate. If you come before I give you permission, you're not going to be allowed to wear anything at all today. I'm planning on introducing you to the rest of my pack today and it's up to you whether you'll be naked when I do it," he warned, and I shook harder.

"Please," I begged.

It terrified me how quickly he could turn me from a proud woman to a soaking wet whimpering mess needy for release.

For several more agonizing moments, he forced me to wait. To me, it felt like forever.

"Please, alpha!"

"Are you going to come long and hard for me, little mate?" he asked.

"Yes! Yes, alpha!"

"Good. Then come for me now, my pretty mate. Come as hard as you can for me," he coaxed.

He didn't have to tell me twice.

My entire body clamped down hard and I let go, finally basking in the ultimate bliss of release. There was no pain this time, only pleasure and it was glorious.

I moaned his name, and his fingers worked my clit even more firmly, dragging out every last second of ecstasy that he could. My thighs quivered. My spine arched hard, pressing my bottom against the very thick and hard length of his cock. It sat snugly between my bottom cheeks, and I blushed hard as the thought of him sliding it inside my bottom hole passed over me.

My orgasm only seemed to strengthen after that.

Fiery scalding hot bliss radiated through me, feeling like a warm beam of light passing over me. The heat blossomed over my heart, wrapping around me like a blanket and when my release finally began to fade, it left me feeling as though I was floating on air.

"Good girl," he whispered, and another electrifying thrill raced straight to my heart.

As the pleasure ebbed away, I hummed softly with satisfaction.

"Thank you," I murmured, and he pressed his lips against my throat. I could tell he was smiling, and it was infectious.

"It was my pleasure, sweet mate. I wanted to make sure you enjoyed waking up in my bed for the first time," he whispered. I giggled a little, a giddy combination of shame, satisfaction, and blissfully sated happiness.

He held me for a few minutes and when my heart stopped racing in my chest, he took me by the hand and led me into his closet. I walked on numb legs, but he was exceedingly patient with me until I was stable on my feet.

"I took the liberty of ordering you a few things before I came for you yesterday. You will find them hanging for you over there," he guided, pointing to the left side rail.

He ordered more than a few things. He'd practically ordered me a wardrobe.

My mouth was slightly agape as I took a step toward what appeared to be at least forty different dresses. Some were a solid color, others covered in a simple hexagonal pattern, and even more consisted of soft flowy fabric decorated with a brilliant variety of brightly colored flowers.

"Pick your favorite and put it on for me. There's shoes for you underneath on the wooden rack," he explained.

"Are there any panties? Or maybe a bra?" I asked, looking around, and a ruthless smile crossed his lips.

"You won't be wearing either today," he answered.

His devilish grin only widened with diabolic intent, and I whined softly.

I don't know why, but his expression made me weak. I couldn't think of anything to say, so I said nothing at all. I looked down at the floor, trying to hide the way a flush of heat was burning up my cheeks. Wearing a dress without any panties beneath it seemed especially shameful and I chewed my lip anxiously knowing with every step I took today, he would know that I was bare underneath my skirt.

Swiftly, he came to me and forced a finger under my chin. He smiled knowingly and I squirmed, feeling my wetness slick against my thighs. I blushed harder, knowing that he could likely smell it. My nipples tightened and I was too proud to make a move to cover them up.

Bastard.

I bet he knew exactly what he was doing to me.

I jerked my head and pulled my chin from his grasp. He smirked, chuckling as he walked over to the other side of the closet. Desperate to cover my naked body, I chose the first garment that called to me, a soft flowy white wrap dress. The fabric was covered in a muted blue rose petal pattern that I liked very much. It wrapped around my waist, and I tied it tight, grateful for any kind of cloth to finally be covering my bare form.

It felt decadently shameful to not be wearing any panties though. I was distinctly aware of the heaviness in my breasts as well, knowing that I was going to feel them shake rather disgracefully with every step. My hard nipples would probably show through the fabric. I tried to put it out of my head, futile as I knew that would be.

I'd be thinking about it all day and the worst part of it all was that it was making me wet.

With a nervous fumble, I found the shoes he'd talked about and slipped my feet into a dark gray quilted pair of ballet flats. They were so soft and cozy, almost like walking on a pillow and I could only guess at what that sort of comfort cost.

When I was done, I turned to face him with a brave face. He'd adorned a black suit with a cream-colored button-up underneath. He was rifling through his ties, and I daringly wandered over, thumbing a burgundy one embroidered with gold thread. It stuck out to me, and I got the sudden urge to see it on him.

"Will you wear this one?" I asked cautiously.

"Gladly," he smiled as he lifted my fingers to his lips. He kissed them softly and I shyly grinned in return. "Thanks for your help," he added.

He went to lift it up over his head himself but paused when my fingers pressed against his wrist.

"Will you allow me?"

"Since you asked so nicely, little one," he answered. I took the tie from his hands and wound it around his neck, tucking it beneath his collar and tying it in a neat square knot. When I was done, he inspected my work in a mirror and cleared his throat approvingly.

"I used to tie my father's all the time. He was the one that taught me," I said quietly.

"He taught you well, Ava," Lawson said. "You did a really nice job."

"Thanks," I grinned.

"Now, let me show you around the house and you can meet a few members of my pack," he said, and a tiny glimmer of excitement raced through me.

"Okay," I replied, and I took his hand when he offered it. He guided me out of his room and with every step, I was reminded of how bare I felt beneath my skirt. I tried to swallow my desire for him to touch me again, but I soon realized there would be none of that.

If he was near, I'd probably be wet forever.

The hallway was quite grand, but at the same time it had a certain southern charm that was quite welcoming. The walls were painted a warm cream color and the dark wood crown molding gave it a rich character that spoke to the home's age. There were some beautiful paintings along the walls that depicted various scenes in the bayou, from sunset to sunrise and everywhere in between. There were even a few renditions of the quarter and I paused by one that had Café Du Monde in the background.

Cautiously, I reached out to touch it, lightly tracing my fingertip across the textured surface. Lawson still held my hand in his and squeezed it in support.

"Together," he murmured.

I didn't answer. I wasn't quite sure what all of this meant for me yet. I was certain of one thing though.

I was going to make the Venuti pay for what they'd done to my father.

When I was ready, I dropped my hand and allowed him to lead me through the rest of the house. He guided me through one guestroom after another as well as a number of extravagantly decorated offices including his own. There were sitting rooms, balcony gardens, and even more guestrooms on the upper floors. It was oddly deserted for such a massive home, but I didn't say anything about it yet. It wasn't until we descended to the ground floor that we came across anyone at all. I blushed and smiled tentatively when I saw who it was.

Toboe was waiting outside a set of carved wooden doors that looked like they belonged at the entryway of a church. He grinned once he saw the two of us and I found that his unending happiness was endearing. I liked him, even if he'd seen his alpha take my virgin asshole for the first time.

I blushed and tried to put my embarrassment out of my mind. Thankfully, Lawson and Toboe started talking to one another, leaving me alone to stew in my own unexpectedly delayed mortification.

"Most of the pack is gathered inside, boss, at least the ones we could spare. I took the liberty of directing a fair number of them to guard the perimeter and stationed more than usual in the quarter. I figured you'd approve," Toboe explained to him.

"I do approve," Lawson answered. "Any recent changes I should know about?"

"No. Not yet," Toboe replied.

"I want to know immediately if you sense anything. I mean it. Anything at all," Lawson commanded.

"You'll be the first to know," Toboe answered, his voice laden with firm resolve.

Lawson nodded once, effectively ending the conversation. He opened the big door, revealing what looked to be a fairly large amphitheater behind them. Most of the seats were filled. There were far more members of the Crescent Moon Pack than I'd anticipated.

The room was circular, and down in the center was a platform with two leather chairs set up almost like a pair of thrones. Lawson began to descend the stairs, striding toward the middle with me in tow. Many of the seats were full, men and women of his pack watching as we walked by. There were small details I noticed as we walked down the aisle; the beautiful hard wood beneath our feet, the molding along the edges as well as the carved handrails along the aisle. The southern charm I'd seen throughout the house wasn't lost in this room and I found that I liked it just as much as the rest.

When we reached the bottom, Lawson sat down in the largest chair and pointed at the one next to him, directing me to sit too. With a bit of trepidation, I sat down beside him, looking out at those gathered in the room with us. Their expressions were ones of curiosity and a mild sense of reservation as they studied me, but I could understand that.

I was a stranger in their midst, and I was sitting right next to their king.

Instead of letting it get to me, I lifted my head with confidence. Lawson cleared his throat, and I crossed my legs as I leaned back against the chair, playing the part of a queen in their midst. It felt kind of nice the longer I embraced it.

"Welcome, pack members," he said, his words echoing loudly all around us. A hush fell over the crowd, and they turned toward him, at least for a minute or two. It didn't take them long to give into temptation and look back at me. I stayed quiet, enjoying the feeling of being encased in mystery, for a little while longer anyway.

"I called you here to talk to you about a few things, the first being some rather precarious developments in our ongoing situation with the Venuti Clan. It appears they've undermined our authority here in the quarter more than any of us have realized for months now, and it's about time we reminded them that the Crescent Moon Pack has just as much, if not more power, than they do," he began.

A cheer rang out over the audience and Lawson waited patiently for them to quiet back down. I glanced from him to the pack, trying to figure out what he had in mind. His pack looked at him with quiet apprehension, but it was overshadowed by an overwhelming sense of loyalty and respect. The more I watched them, the more I could see that they both loved and feared him. I don't know why, but I decided that I liked that.

"Unbeknownst to them however, I have a secret weapon that may very well be the key to their downfall. Everyone, I want you to meet my mate, Ava Winters," Lawson continued. His pronouncement was a bit irksome, but I swallowed it down.

I noticed some movement at the back of the room, and I watched as Toboe entered through the big set of wooden doors. He stood at the back of the aisle and observed over the proceedings, his gaze passing over the excited members of his pack at the announcement that their alpha had found his mate.

Lawson glanced at me, and we locked eyes for just a moment, but it was enough to send my body into a tailspin of desire.

My nipples pebbled and I pressed my palms against my thighs in an effort to keep my arousal at bay. It was frustrating not having control over my own body and it was starting to infuriate me.

"As your alpha, I demand that you show her the same deference and loyalty that you give me. She may be human, but she is also my mate," he continued. "I expect every single one of you to respect that."

His possessiveness left me unsettled, balanced somewhere on the edge of annoyance and desire. There was a burning sort of fury brewing inside me and I couldn't seem to keep it at bay. He kept speaking and I wondered if he was going to allow me to say anything about what I was here for. I didn't like it, but I swallowed that feeling, deciding to just let him continue to speak.

At least for now.

"She has the capability to create a rather special, very advanced weapon that is extremely effective against the Venuti, and she is going to share that with all of us," he said next, and my fury exploded.

The fuck I was. That knowledge was mine and I wasn't about to begin sharing it.

There was no containing myself now, no biting my lip and keeping myself quiet. I was going to tell him exactly how I felt, and he was going to listen to every word I said. I didn't much care if he liked any of it either.

Sure, he may insist on calling me his mate and I couldn't change how my body was continually responding to his presence, but that didn't mean I was going to share my father's work with him.

I didn't need him or his pack. I'd only ever needed myself and that wasn't going to change just because I bore his mark on my neck.

"That was never a part of the plan, Lawson. I don't need your help and I'm certainly not going to give away my father's life-work to you and your pack. I can handle the Venuti myself," I declared proudly.

The room went silent. The tension was thick enough to cut with a knife and I could have sworn everyone in the audience stopped breathing. Lawson cleared his throat, and I lifted my chin even higher in defiance. My palms felt oddly sweaty, and I squeezed my fingers into tight little fists in order to try to ignore it.

"No. You won't, little mate. You're going to teach all of us how to make your sunfire bullets and we are going to make sure the Venuti never treads on our territory again. We're going to do it together, as a pack," he replied. His words were thick with warning, and I knew that I was angering him. To be honest, I didn't much care.

I was too wet, too needy, and far too angry to listen to the small voice of reason in the back of my head.

"You may have forced me to be your mate, but that doesn't mean I'm going to obey your every command. I didn't choose to be a part of your pack. You can't order me around like a dog," I retorted, making sure that he could hear the defiance in every syllable that came out of my mouth.

He sighed, and it made my stomach drop precipitously to my toes. With a deep breath, I tried to remain brave as he pushed himself out of the seat, but even that began to waver as he walked toward me. I didn't run. Maybe I should have in that moment, but by the time he grasped my upper arm and pulled me out of my own chair it was far too late.

I gritted my teeth, firmly setting my mouth in a thin line as I pulled every ounce of brazen courage inside me that I could manage. His eyes were dark, glinting with unspoken warning. The first tendril of regret played at my heart as his fingers tightened just enough to pull me back toward his seat.

With his other hand, he swiftly untied the wrap dress and roughly pulled it open. I fought him, but his movements were faster as he forced it down the length of my arm. Quickly, he grasped my other arm and did the same on the other side, baring me swiftly and effectively before I could do anything to stop it.

He'd stripped me in front of his entire pack.

After he was finished, he stood there and just let the fact that I was completely naked sink in. My ability to speak words flew out the window and I tried to move to cover myself, but he quickly pinned my arms behind my back, putting all of my body on display for his pack. He forced me to look out at the crowd and my tongue went dry. I could see them watching me, looking up and down my body with open interest and a soft keening whine escaped my throat.

"It is unfortunate that your introduction to my pack had to go this way, little mate," he purred, and my body revolted.

My nipples pebbled and a single drop of wetness slid down the expanse of my right inner thigh.

"Your feisty nature has a time and a place, Ava, but now is not it. I am alpha of this pack, and no one questions my authority, not even you. I do not tolerate defiance and you will be punished, but since you refused me in front of everyone here, they all are going to watch as you learn a very shameful lesson," he warned, and I froze.

He couldn't mean that.

I tried to rip my hands from his grasp, but his grip was too strong. I bent forward, attempting to throw him over my shoulder even though he was more than twice my size. Not surprisingly, that didn't work either. I tried every maneuver that I knew, but nothing was enough to free me from his hold.

He kicked my seat out of the way and while holding me firmly with one hand, moved the other into the center of the platform. I tried to take advantage of that single moment, but he moved too quickly and before I knew it, he was sitting down and pulling me toward him. He released my wrists and took hold of my hand, jerking me forward hard enough to make me lose my balance and fall face down over his lap.

He was going to spank me in front of everyone.

I struggled hard once that realization hit me, but he was prepared for that. Without ceremony, he tipped me forward and forced a leg over the back of one of mine. The effect of the position was instantaneous, putting everything in between my thighs on display for everyone to see. With one hand, he pinned me to his lap and no matter how much I pushed at his leg beneath my hips, I didn't budge the slightest bit.

"You already know that the scent of your arousal is especially enticing to me, but you should know that the rest of my pack can smell it too. All of us knew you were wet before I put you over my knee, but now all of us can see just how soaked that naughty little pussy is, can't they, little mate?" he asked.

I cried out in dismay.

He swatted between my legs firmly, sending a stinging frisson of pain radiating across my sensitive folds. I tried to squeeze my thighs shut, but his leg prevented that. Instead, I managed to kick my other leg, yet it did nothing to make him let me go. I stopped moving once I realized I was just exposing myself even more when I did that.

"Answer me, mate," he demanded sternly, and I growled in frustration.

His hand settled on my backside, still and threatening all the same.

"Don't!" I screeched and he spanked my bottom hard, causing my right cheek to jiggle just enough to expose the entirety of my pussy to those watching. He did the same to the left side and I vowed that I wouldn't make a sound, no matter how hard he spanked me.

I should have known better.

His hand was ruthlessly cruel. He spanked me with purpose, wanting to punish me and maybe on some level, to break me so that he could teach me a lesson for undermining him in front of his pack. He punished up and down my thighs, over every square inch of my backside and he even used his hands to spread open my bottom cheeks so he could spank there too. Those were especially hard, and I struggled to take them, but I didn't have much of a choice.

From the very start, he spanked me so hard that it felt as if my ass had caught fire. Every smack smoldered and sizzled with stinging pain. Prickles of sharp agony blossomed across each cheek, spreading and settling inward until it reached the center of my core. My pussy quivered and I knew that I was getting wetter the longer this went on.

I wanted to beg him to stop, but I kept my mouth shut. The punishing bite of his hand never lessened, but he eventually paused long enough for me to catch my breath. I renewed my vow to keep quiet, banking on my inner courage to help me keep it.

"I expect a proper answer, little mate," he demanded. I refused to give him one.

"Fuck you," I said instead. I don't know why I continued to challenge him, and I don't know where I found the bravery to do it, but I did.

The sound of his pack gasping in shock was audible and my insides twisted in sudden anxiety. I whimpered quietly, actively regretting the words immediately after they left my mouth. They had been foolishly brazen, and I knew at once that I was going to pay dearly for them.

"Toboe. Do me the honor of fetching a wooden spoon from the kitchen, please," Lawson called out.

"You got it, boss," Toboe answered with far too much glee.

"No!" I shrieked, but Lawson cut me off before I could finish.

"Little mate, you should know I will thoroughly take you in hand no matter where we are or who we are with. I will deal with you properly whenever you need it. Right now, you need your bare little bottom spanked hard with a wooden spoon until you're sobbing over my knee. That should make you nervous, but the part that should really make you nervous is going to come after that," he declared, and a hot shiver raced down my spine.

"You can't," I gasped.

"I can and I will. You need to be punished and I intend to do exactly that," he said darkly.

"You don't have to do this," I said softly, trying to volley for his mercy even though I knew the chances of him taking the bait were slim to none.

Instead of answering right away, he slipped his fingers between my thighs, and I gasped. I was immediately ashamed of just how easily his thick digits slid along my slick folds and of how everyone watching could see him touch me like that.

"Ava, you're protesting an awful lot for a little girl with a pussy this soaking wet," he observed and the heat that had been creeping along my face very nearly exploded with sizzling intensity.

I heard the wooden doors open and close. Toboe's footsteps echoed as he jogged down the stairs and joined us. Lawson's fingers pulled away from my pussy and soon enough, the cool surface of the spoon pressed against my backside.

I couldn't shake the overwhelming sense of doom that was about to rain down on me.

He tapped the spoon lightly against my bottom and a soft sound of quiet nervousness escaped me. He popped my right cheek gently, but the resulting sting was enough to catch me off guard. Maybe I was right to fear it.

"I'm going to enjoy reminding you of your place very much, little mate, but I'm quite certain you're not going to feel the same way," he murmured, and I jerked hard just before the spoon connected with my left cheek much harder than the warning tap he'd threatened me with before.

The sting was instantaneous, but far sharper and more overwhelming than his hand or even his belt. A cry escaped my lips and I slammed them back together, trying to swallow the sound. Another hard spank with the spoon followed on the opposite side, harsh and ruthless and it was then that my punishment truly began.

There was nothing other than my naked bottom and that dreadful spoon. My world became one with the vicious pain that radiated across my entire backside with every cruel spank. He left no spot unpunished, thoroughly disciplining the entire expanse of my cheeks and my thighs. He even spread open my bottom and exposed me to the crowd as he used the spoon to punish the inside of my cleft. I shrieked at the intense sting, trying to take it with dignity, but I was quickly losing that. I'd broken my vow.

I don't know how long I lasted without making a sound, but it didn't much matter really. That spoon was vicious, and I fought him with every breath, trying to squirm and escape its bite. I never did. That spoon met its mark every time, cruel and brutal, and as it continued, I began to feel like I was losing control.

He had taken that control and he wasn't letting go.

He started to punish the lower curve of my bottom and the tops of my thighs even harder than before, and my breath caught in the back of my throat. I blinked several times as I tried to stop the inevitable, but I knew it was a losing battle. My eyes watered and no matter what I did to try to hold it back, the first tear dripped down my cheek of its own accord. Another followed. Then another, until a volley of tears stained my cheeks.

As I sobbed, it was as if the fight had drained out of me. I no longer kicked or fought. The spanks still came, harsh and mean, but they'd also started to slow. Eventually, he stopped, and I was left to suffer the full stinging weight of the aftermath of that dreaded spoon. I was still though, suffering with my red bottom on display.

"Open your legs, little mate. You have three more to take on that naughty little pussy," he commanded. I sobbed harder, but I obeyed. I was showcasing myself to the audience and I knew they would be able to see just how wet my punishment had made me, but it didn't much matter. My alpha had given me an instruction and I needed to follow it.

Fearfully, I spread my thighs as much as I could. He placed the back of the spoon against the bare lips of my pussy.

"These are going to hurt, mate, but I want you to always remember to follow your alpha's command. I want you to remember how sore your pussy was after you defied me. Do you understand me?" he pressed.

"Yes, alpha," I whispered fearfully, yet at the same time my inner walls fluttered with need.

"You will count them for me, pretty mate," he continued, and I shivered hard. My whole world centered between my thighs, focused entirely on the back of that spoon spanking my pussy bright red.

The first one took my breath away. The sharp, cruel sting was so much more than I expected, radiating across my sensitive flesh. The vicious bite lasted far longer than I was prepared for and only after several seconds did it began to abate.

A brutal wave of pleasure followed.

"One, alpha," I finally managed. My voice was hoarse and shaky with fright.

The second one was even harder.

I whimpered through the aftermath, trying to be brave and take what he wanted to give me, but suffering all the same. The sting was brighter, but the desire that came after was even fiercer.

"Two, alpha," I breathed.

The third was hardest of all.

I screamed, my voice breaking with several whining cries as the pain blossomed across my pussy. The pain was harsh and swift, much more than all the rest and I struggled to take it. A fresh wave of tears dripped down my cheeks.

The need that followed that last punishing spank was the roughest part. With tears streaming down my cheeks, I realized that the only thing I wanted was his cock sinking deep into my pussy, ravaging me, taking me and making me fall apart all over it.

The spoon clattered to the floor and his fingers dipped in between my thighs.

"I know what you need, little mate, but I want you to ask me for it. You will make sure that everyone hears it too, even those sitting in the back of the room," my alpha commanded.

I whined in shame.

I opened my mouth, once, twice before I clamped it shut. His fingers continued to tease me, circling around my clit. I didn't just want his fingers. I wanted his cock.

"What do you need, little mate?" he pressed.

"I need you to fuck me, alpha," I said, the words flying out of my mouth unprecedented. I couldn't do anything about them now that they were out in the open. I'd spoken out loud and he'd heard me.

"Louder," he demanded.

"Please. Will you fuck me, alpha?" I cried out, doing my best to be as loud as I could. My face heated with sizzling fire and for once, I was happy to be face down over his knee so that no one could see just how embarrassed I was.

He didn't answer. Instead, he lifted me off his lap and bent me over the back of the chair.

"Place your hands on the seat. I'm going to fuck you right here, little mate, and everyone is going to watch you break on my cock," he said darkly, and my pussy squeezed tight.

I couldn't contain the arousal that surged through me at the knowledge that I was going to get fucked.

In public.

And everyone was going to see it.

As I struggled with my fear, raging mortification, and primal arousal, I didn't hear him undo his belt. I wasn't ready for his cock to slam into me, but my body opened for him nonetheless.

It hurt from the very start.

He was so big, so thick that no matter how many times he fucked me, I knew that it was always going to leave me sore. My pussy stretched wide, and his entry burned hot. Despite all that, my inner walls clutched greedily at him, and I sighed in relief at the sensation of fullness.

He'd been right. I'd wanted this. I'd needed this.

His fingers wound in the hair at the back of my head, and he clutched it tight, forcing a blooming flower of pain to spread across my scalp. He made me look straight into the faces of everyone watching.

"When you come for me, I want everyone to see it. I want them to see the beauty of my mate's face when she comes on her alpha's cock," he demanded, and my pussy squeezed tight around him.

I wondered if he was going to make me come more than once. Something deep inside me hoped that he would.

He thrust into me so hard that I feared the chair would fall over. It didn't though. It was strong, steady, and it didn't move an inch no matter how hard his cock viciously pistoned into my pussy.

Already sore and very well punished from the wooden spoon, my ability to keep myself under control was long gone. My orgasm brewed with a terrifying swiftness. My alpha had spanked me for a very real reason in front of his entire pack and that was making it difficult to fight the rising tide of arousal in my veins.

I cried out and my voice was hoarse with need.

"Beg me for permission, little mate. Don't make me spank that wet little pussy again," he growled.

My response was immediate because I was already so desperate.

"Please, alpha. Please let me come," I begged.

"Do you really want to come, bright red bottom and soaking wet pussy on display? Do you really want to come with everyone watching?" he asked.

"Yes, alpha! Please!" I keened.

I was so close to losing control. I needed to come, and I desperately wanted to avoid another lesson with that awful wooden spoon between my thighs. My legs were shaking, and my nipples were so hard that the feeling of them against the leather of the chair was driving me insane.

His grip on my hair tightened as he forced me to look out at the members of his pack. Every thrust felt harder, faster, and I pleaded even more.

"Please. Please," I murmured.

"Come for me, little mate. Scream for me so loud that everyone watching can see you break for your alpha," he ordered.

My orgasm crashed over me at his words.

I writhed, pushing my hips back and taking him deeper. Every part of me convulsed around his massive cock, milking him and taking all that he gave me. My arousal was hot and heavy from the start, all-consuming and I found myself drowning in the intensity of it.

At first, I was quiet, taking my release in silence before I couldn't help it any longer. I started to moan and just a few moments after that I began to scream.

Exquisitely hot bliss poured over me, surging through my veins in hot steady pulses that threatened to never end. That orgasm was deeply satisfying in a way I'd never known, beautiful and dangerous and far more taboo than anything I'd ever felt before.

This was filthy and I loved it.

The best part was that he showed no signs of slowing down. He was going to make me come again and I wasn't going to be able to do a thing about it.

I got hotter, my bliss stronger, and I thrashed beneath him. I stopped thinking about how embarrassed I was to be getting fucked before the pack and started to shamelessly give into each and every thrust. My hips rocked back, and I lifted my bottom up as he slammed into me, taking him deeper than ever.

My core ballooned outward with pleasure, curling and twisting with every passing second, filling with unmatched desire so much so that I knew my next orgasm was already imminent.

My fingers grasped at the seat of the chair, tightening at the edges as I tried to hold on to the wild ride that was coming for him time and time again. My thighs trembled and a needy wail came from my lips unbidden.

His hand tightened in my hair and that was all I needed to fall apart on his cock once again. I'm not sure how he did it, but he toyed with my body as if I was a musical instrument that only he knew how to play.

I quaked hard and my world fractured. My eyes rolled back in my head as his grasp on my hips tightened, holding me up when my legs shook hard enough so that I wasn't sure if I was even capable of standing anymore. My toes curled and everything inside me tightened into a pleasurable little ball, exploding outward and coming together in one beautiful display of fiery passion.

This was perfection.

That second orgasm faded, and I hesitantly realized that it still wasn't over. His thrusts got harder, more persistent, and I realized then that he was using me for his own pleasure now.

"You've got one more orgasm, little mate," he demanded, and my heart pounded with a sense of panic.

The first two orgasms had been so strong that there was no doubt in my mind that this final one was going to be the hardest of all to take. I also knew on some level it was going to hurt quite a bit.

He pounded into me so roughly that I knew it would leave me sore for some time after this was all over. That only served to make me burn hotter, moan louder, and made my need swirl inside me with fervor once again.

"Oh, please, alpha," I begged.

"You will ask for permission before that orgasm, mate," he commanded and I whimpered softly, taking every last inch of his cock and burning for more.

I drifted along that wave of pleasure for as long as I was able until all at once it became too much. It was as if I was riding the tallest roller coaster in existence and that dreaded fall was just fractions of a second away. There was no stopping what was coming and that made it all the more frightening and arousing all at the same time.

"Please let me come, alpha," I pleaded.

He was silent for a few moments, and I panicked a little, unsure if I would be able to hold myself back for much longer. I feared disobeying him at the same time that it aroused me, and I wasn't sure which one would win out in the end.

I begged for him shamelessly.

"Please. I can't take any more, alpha. Please. I'm sorry I disobeyed you. Please have mercy. Please let me come for you," I cried. My voice was pitifully needy, shaking and weak and more than a little broken.

"Have you learned your lesson not to defy your alpha, mate?" he pressed.

"Yes, alpha," I keened, so desperate and frantic that I almost didn't recognize myself.

"You may come for me now, mate. Come hard for your alpha while he marks your pretty little cunt with his seed," he roared and the first blazing hot surge of his seed pelted against my inner walls, driving me mad and forcing that next orgasm over me without warning.

I screamed hard once more, shaking and shivering and losing all of myself with my alpha's cock deep inside me. His cum continued to spurt inside me, fiery tendrils of his need and mine combined. I shook and trembled, shamelessly writhing beneath him as I took everything he had to give me.

The pleasure was soon overwhelmed by a wave of pain. At first it was viciously ruthless in its intensity, but it soon molded into the passionate need raging on inside me. Pain and pleasure came together into a single endless sensation that left me quivering and entirely captive in its terribly wonderful embrace.

My inner walls clutched greedily at his length, taking him as deep as he could go. I could feel his seed spurting against my cervix, burning hot and utterly possessive. With every single one, my orgasm compounded on itself, marking me as his so thoroughly that I would be forever changed. I could fight it all I want, but that didn't change the truth.

I loved him.

As my orgasm raged on, he turned my head just enough so that he could capture my lips in a brutal kiss that left them sore. He kissed me roughly enough that I knew I would feel it long after, but as those final moments of my release tore through me, my heart beat for him.

Only for him.

When that orgasm finally began to ebb away, my entire body felt numb. My pussy throbbed intermittently, reminding me of what had just happened and making me blush because of it. He groaned and released my hair at last, sliding out of me and gathering me in his arms immediately. I was hardly aware of Toboe passing Lawson a blanket, but as it wrapped around me, I shivered with appreciation.

Lawson sat back down in the chair I'd just gotten fucked over and pulled me into his lap.

For a period of time, we were quiet. His pack watched in silence, and I pressed my head against his shoulder, basking in the protection the warmth of his body was providing. I floated for a while, somewhere in the midst of shame and thorough satisfaction at the events that had just taken place in this room.

"Good girl," he whispered, and my breath caught in the back of my throat.

His thumb traced across my cheek lightly, back and forth. It was hypnotic in a way, and I quickly decided that it was the most incredible caress I'd ever had the pleasure of experiencing.

I whimpered softly and he hugged me tighter.

"Shhh. There's my good girl. I've got you now. You're safe with me. You'll always be safe with your alpha," he purred.

His voice captivated me, and I closed my eyes, exhausted.

"Rest now, little mate. We'll come up with a plan for the Venuti later," he murmured.

"I love you," I answered. I hadn't meant to say the words, but they just fell out of me. I couldn't have stopped them even if I knew they were coming.

"I love you too, Ava. From the first moment I saw you, I've loved you."

CHAPTER 9

Lawson

I conducted the rest of that meeting with a very tired and satisfied mate in my arms. She slept while I informed my pack of the many times the Venuti had come into our territory, from the times they'd killed when they weren't supposed to, to the killing and siring of the governor's daughter, to the story of what they'd done to Ava's father.

"My mate Ava had an important part of her family taken away from her by the Venuti, but they took it a step further. They turned her family name into one of a villain's. Her father will always be known as a monster, and that's something that she deserves to get closure for," I explained, and I could see the angry grimaces that came from her story. Even Toboe looked down at her with fury for what she'd already gone through, his mouth set in a firm line.

"Together, we're going to make sure the Venuti pay for what they did to her. I want to see them burn," I vowed. Toboe grinned wickedly. Beside him, Tara whooped in excitement.

I'd never allowed them to really go after the Venuti, no holds barred. I was ready to let them now. They'd caused my mate pain and they were going to suffer for it.

"I want full scale weapons production. You will work from sunup to sundown and everywhere in between. Take shifts. Pair off and make sure that everything is going as planned. I don't want delays of any kind. I believe that the Venuti are going to come for us, and I want us ready. I want us to be able to destroy them the moment they step into our territory," I declared.

It was time for action now. The Venuti were going to step right into a trap, and I was going to look forward to the look on their faces when they realized how fucked they were. I grinned, feeling wickedly excited to know that time was coming. It had been a long time since I'd engaged with any of the other families in a battle like this, and I was going to enjoy every moment of it.

My pack applauded. They screamed and howled with contagious excitement, and I grinned even wider.

"Get ready. We're going to war," I roared over the noise of my pack, and they cheered so much louder. They started clapping and some of them even started to pound their feet against the floor.

This was going to be fun.

* * *

Over the next three weeks, my mansion turned into a factory for sunfire bullets and wooden stakes. Ava had blossomed under my watch and that of my pack. Her resistance in sharing her father's work had fully melted away, and she took an incredible amount of time in teaching us all how to create the bullets her father had invented. The more time I spent with her, the more I realized how intelligent she was. I also came to understand just how big a heart she had.

Any animosity she'd had toward my kind had all but disappeared. She befriended a number of my pack members, including Toboe, a sweet but very shy beta named Sasha, as well as several others. She even laughed and played with some of the children, letting them put tiaras on her head and reading them stories late into the night when they came calling for her.

In no time at all, she felt like a member of my family and that made my heart swell even more for her than it already had.

I watched her interact with my pack and when she went off to work on the production one night, I followed her. From afar, I observed her and grinned, just enjoying the way everyone around her seemed to smile with her in the room.

She gave a few orders for items, and I narrowed my eyes in curiosity. Unable to keep my inquisitiveness at bay, I strode over to her in silence, making her jump when my hands caressed along her hips.

"Lawson!" she squeaked in surprise.

"What are you up to, little mate?" I purred and I was delighted when a beautifully pink blush colored her cheeks. She stammered for a second and I pressed a soft kiss against the side of her neck, making her lose her words for a little bit longer. I decided I liked that very much. When she was finally able to gather herself enough to speak, I allowed it, knowing that there would be many more times where I'd be able to stoke her desire just through words alone.

"I had an idea," she began. Her eyes sparkled and I decided I liked that very much too.

"Tell me about it," I urged.

"Wooden bullets aren't the most stable, but they're particularly good at weakening a vampire because they tend to splinter once they hit them. If the wood was soaked in garlic and there was a metal pin driven through the center of the bullet, it would make the bullet more effective," she explained and I couldn't be prouder of her.

"That sounds like a great idea, Ava," I said, hugging her close to me. She smiled broadly, but it seemed to wilt not long after. I didn't say anything yet, deciding to let her speak on her terms.

"I want to fight them, Lawson," she began.

"I know you do, Ava. Did you think that I would keep you from that fight?" I questioned softly, dragging my fingers along the edges of her brow.

"I thought you might," she pouted quite prettily. I had to admit that it was sort of cute.

"I wouldn't take that away from you, pretty mate. In fact, I want you to be at my side in battle," I told her, and I could immediately feel a sense of relief pass over her.

"You really mean that?" she asked.

"I do."

"On your first full day in my mansion, little one, I commissioned a special set of battle armor just for you. My pack and I have our own protection, but your human body does not. I ensured that it would be light enough not to hinder your ability to move or fight, but it will protect you from what the vampires might attack us with. It won't stop a bullet entirely, but it will slow it down enough to ensure that you don't end up too gravely injured if you're hit," I continued.

"Really?" she asked.

"It was never my intention to limit your fire, Ava. It's one of the things I love so much about you," I assured her.

Without warning, she twisted around and pressed her lips against mine in a sweet kiss. Her mouth was so soft and inviting, raw temptation in a feisty little package. I wanted so much more of it.

"I love you," she purred. "I didn't think I'd ever come to love someone like you, but now that I have you, I'm looking forward to spending the rest of my days with you."

She made me weak, but at the same time she made me so incredibly strong. I would fight harder for her so that I could protect her and keep her safe. Her wants and desires had become mine and I was going to use every day to show her exactly that.

"I love you forever and for always, my pretty mate," I answered, and I couldn't help but kiss her again. She melted in my embrace and almost reluctantly, I pulled back and gently lifted her chin with my finger.

"Go upstairs to our bedroom. Your armor is waiting there. Put it on, I want to see it on you," I instructed quietly. She shivered and I grazed my thumb over top of the mark on her neck. It had long healed over, leaving a beautiful white scar that told the world she was mine and mine alone. She sucked her lower lip into her mouth, her breathing quickly becoming short and uneven.

"Yes, alpha," she answered, and the scent of her arousal was suddenly thick in the air. My pack was polite enough not to show that they noticed, but I knew that they did. They knew their alpha could make his mate wet with nothing but a few words and that knowledge made my cock rock hard. She rushed up the stairs and took off in the direction of our bedroom and I leaned against the wall, crossing my arms over my chest and waiting for her to return.

I didn't expect Toboe to come rushing to my side instead.

"Boss, I think we might have a situation," he exclaimed, and he stopped long enough to sniff the air. "I regret to inform you that you'll probably have to deal with your mate at another time because I'm fairly certain we're going to have several uninvited guests to contend with very shortly…"

I sighed with annoyance, knowing what he meant but that didn't make my cock any less hard.

"Do those visitors happen to have a pointy set of fangs?" I growled, more than a little irritated at the timing of those that would come to challenge us. I resisted the urge to race upstairs and fuck my pretty mate senseless. With a sigh, I turned toward him and ignored the iron spike between my legs.

"Yes. They entered the quarter just a few minutes ago. There are at least two hundred of them, maybe more, walking the streets in our direction," he replied.

I glanced out the window, taking note that the sun had just set on the horizon. With no direct sunlight now, they could walk outside with freedom. They had all night to meet us in battle, at least until the sun rose the next morning.

I'd already taken precautions and gathered much of my pack in my mansion. Even with more than a dozen guestrooms, there were people sleeping on the floor, on couches, and a number of cots strewn all throughout the house. The children as well as the sick and elderly were gathered at the center of the house so that we would be able to protect them no matter what. They would be the last to fall prey to the Venuti, but I would fight tooth and nail to keep them from even getting close.

"Make the call. Get everyone up and on the perimeter. I want everyone armed to the teeth. Spare nothing. The Venuti are cocky enough so that they think they can take us, but we were going to show them that they have vastly underestimated us."

"Got it, boss," Toboe answered. His sarcasm had gone, and he was serious now. He knew the risks that tonight's battle was going to bring, and his strength was starting to show. He was my beta, second only to me.

"Oh, and Toboe?"

He paused and turned back toward me.

"Bring me the weapons I had built for both me and Ava. All of them," I commanded.

"Right away, boss," he answered.

CHAPTER 10

Ava

I descended the stairs two at a time. I'd put on every piece of armor that Lawson had made for me, enjoying how it all fit me almost too perfectly. I wore a thin cotton shirt and stretchy pants beneath the dark leather pieces, but the bullet-proof vest was the most impressive part of the whole thing.

I could feel a thin layer of Kevlar inside it, but there was a layer of flexible steel spirals encased within it too. I thought it would hinder my movement when I'd first picked it up, but when I'd slipped it over my head and strapped it around my waist, it did anything but. It was so well contoured to my shape and it moved with me; I felt all the more powerful in it.

When I walked down the stairs though, the mansion had erupted into a flurry of activity that could only mean one thing.

The Venuti were on their way.

Lawson strode through the foyer toward me with purpose. He held a black leather case in his hands, and I looked at him with interest. He cocked his head toward the kitchen and by the time I made it to his side, he had it spread open on the table. He picked up a belt and lashed it around my waist without a word. When it was firmly in place, he picked up a gun.

"This is for you. I had one of the best gun makers in the States put it together for you. It won't jam, not even once. It's single fire, so make every shot count," he said as he slid in a fully loaded clip of sunfire bullets. He picked up several more clips and placed them in holsters all along the belt for me, along with a second fully loaded gun.

"Slide your hands along the belt. Take note of the places where I put the clips for you. Do that now, little mate," he instructed.

Slowly, I did as I was bidden, familiarizing myself with each clip along my belt. Next, he flipped a couple of wooden stakes into his grasp and started pushing them into place along my belt too.

"Take note of the stakes as well. Make sure you know where they are so when you need them, you'll be ready," he commanded.

I did as instructed, slowly feeling the smooth base of the sharpened stakes.

"I have one last gift for you. I discussed your sunfire bullets with Genzo, who has a mind like yours that is geared toward innovation. He created something just for you," Lawson explained. He lifted his arm, holding a thick, very sharp knife in his grasp. "Using similar technology to that developed your sunfire bullets, he made you a sunfire blade. In order to use it, you must bury the blade in all the way to the hilt in your target. That alone will not kill them, but when you press on the release on the bottom here, it will activate and blast the unlucky vampire apart. This will only work once, so use it wisely."

He passed the blade to me, and I looked at it in wonder. The button in question was on the bottom of the hilt, and I lightly passed my thumb over it. I nodded my head once, showing him that I understood.

"There is a hidden holster inside your vest for it, here," he continued. Carefully, he took the knife from my fingers and slid it inside an opening just above my belt line. It fit perfectly, likely made to the knife's exact specifications.

"I can't believe you had this all made for me," I sighed softly.

"I take care of my mate, no matter what she needs and today, she needs to take out her revenge on the pointy toothed fuckers that tarnished her family name," he growled.

His words invoked the fire I'd put aside for weeks. I'd focused on building up the members of my pack, on teaching them how to make weapons that would give them an edge over the vampires they would fight against and just generally finding my way in my newfound family.

I lifted my eyes to his, finally allowing a small grin to edge at the corners of my lips.

"Abso-fucking-lutely," I answered, giving into every ounce of animosity I felt against the Venuti. It was their fault I'd lost my father and they were going to pay for that.

He shifted beside me, echoing my sentiments with a growl more vicious than I could have even imagined. I was grateful it wasn't directed at me because I wouldn't want to face something like that. Instead of fighting against him though, he was at my side. The bond between us fluttered at the knowledge that we were going to battle against the Venuti as one.

"I'm proud of you, Ava. Fight hard and make them pay for what they did."

Lawson's voice echoed inside my head. I turned, studying the expression on his wolf face.

"I can hear you," I whispered. His eyes darkened and I could have sworn he was smiling at me, the corners of his mouth lifting up in a toothy grin that looked more like a snarl than anything else.

"We're bonded, my beautiful mate. You bear my mark now and that means that even as a wolf, we are never truly apart. I will hear you wherever you are. Don't be afraid to call for me if you need me."

My heart swelled.

People began to rush by. Men and women alike were loading clips and sliding them into place before they cocked their guns.

"Is there a safety on my gun?" I asked.

"No."

"Good."

"Come. I have the perfect place for you to rain down fire on our enemies."

Without thinking, I swung myself up onto Lawson's back. He turned the corner and rushed up one staircase after the next until he burst out onto the roof. Several members of his pack followed, remaining in human form as they did so. We fanned out across the roof, with Lawson and me taking our place at the center. By the time everyone had settled into their positions, I counted at least two dozen pack members spread out evenly along the roofline.

I looked out and a quiet squeak of momentary fear escaped me I saw just how many of them were coming for us.

There were at least two hundred. Maybe even two hundred and fifty.

"Don't fret, mate. I have you by my side and that makes us far stronger than them."

That single thread of fright withered away, and I gave it no more thought. My brave nature reared its head and with confidence, I pulled both loaded guns from my waist. I took aim and held for my alpha's cue to fire.

"When you're ready, give the command, Ava. Today, the Crescent Moon Pack follows you."

My heart exploded in my chest. I'd fought against him so hard, but he'd conquered me in the end. I loved this man. I would love him to my last dying breath.

I leveled the guns, making sure to aim carefully and I pulled the triggers. With smooth precision, the bullets tore out of the barrel and sailed straight into the skulls of the two unfortunate vampires caught in my sights. In an explosion of light, their heads imploded. If I had the time, I would have admired that small victory, but I quickly moved onto the next. All around me, guns started to fire, and a significant number of the Venuti began to erupt into a fiery display of light, blood, and gore.

Gunfire popped all around me and when I'd unloaded the ten rounds in my clip, I released the empty ones and swiftly replaced them with the full ones on my belt.

Then the Venuti started firing back.

I watched in horror as men who I had befriended were shot beside me. I knew that the vampires were shooting them with silver bullets and that they probably wouldn't get back up. With vicious intent, I leveled my gun on them and kept shooting, not willing to back down for even a second. Every bullet counted and I took out as many as I could. I was the best shot up here and soon enough, I ran out of bullets.

Someone else rushed to my side and handed me two fully loaded clips. I reloaded and took aim, but the vampires were getting so much closer, and it soon became clear that they were coming from all sides.

Fuck...

My first estimate had been far too low. Now I was certain that the Venuti had brought more than five hundred vampires with them. The pack members on the roof continued to pick away at them and reinforcements continued to bring more clips up to them. Quickly, I dismounted Lawson and rushed to the other side of the mansion, trying to pick off those that were scaling the walls. I was able to stop a number of them, but we had been so focused on the incoming horde that we hadn't remembered to check our backs.

They were starting to gain on us. From the perimeter of the property, a rush of wolves tore into the back of the vampires. They caught them off guard, ripping a number of vampires' heads from their torsos before they turned around and began firing into them. Several wolves were hit, and I prayed that they wouldn't be fatal. If the bullets hit in places that weren't vital, they could be removed and if the wolf was lucky, he or she would survive.

I kept firing and when I ran out of bullets, Lawson kicked a few more magazines in my direction. When I finished those, I climbed onto his back, and he leapt off the roof and landed on his feet several stories below. I wrapped my hands around the stakes at my waist and pulled them free, slamming the first into the vampire nearest to me as I leapt off Lawson's back. I sank that stake deep into the vampire heart and yanked it out as he fell to the ground in a heap.

I fought hard, twisting and turning and ignoring the sweat that was dripping down my brow from the southern heat. Lawson stayed by my side, ripping into one vampire after the next with his teeth. He moved so quickly that the vampires he fought against never stood a chance. They couldn't even get their guns up fast enough to take aim before he tore their heads off at the neck.

Had I not been fighting for my own life, I would have stopped to admire him.

From up above, some of the shifters lifted the heavier weaponry I'd designed myself. I smirked when I saw the barrels of the semi-automatic machine guns come into sight, knowing that they were loaded with the wooden bullets soaked in garlic oil. The constant popping sounds of their gunfire went off and the vampires on the battlefield with me screeched in surprise.

They hadn't been expecting that.

I fought on even harder, my confidence renewed. I spun and sank my stake into more vampires than I could count. I made every single step count. I maneuvered with purpose, dancing through the ranks of vampires as if I'd been made for this.

"Keep going, Ava. Keep making me proud."

With a roar, I launched off my feet and stabbed a rather large vamp with my stake. He was so muscled that my stake didn't quite sink in far enough, but Lawson threw his body upward, using the base of his paw to slam the wooden weapon in far enough to kill him. I stared down at it for a second, almost in surprise.

I wouldn't be able to wrench that one back out.

I reached for my belt and grabbed another. The continual blast of gunfire from above was comforting. A vampire sped toward me, and I sidestepped to avoid him, only to have the contents of his skull explode across my cheek. I hastily wiped it off of me, knowing it was probably still streaked across my face.

I turned back, only to see Toboe about twenty feet away, a lopsided grin on his face.

"Thanks!" I called out.

"No problem, boss lady," he answered and in seconds, he'd shifted back into his wolf form only to tear into another vampire. His fighting style was rather majestic, smooth and swift, almost as if he was dancing through the battlefield. I didn't watch him for long, because I was quickly distracted by another vampire rushing my way. I clocked him in the jaw hard and spun fast, feinting in one direction before I stepped back and slammed my stake straight into his heart. He was thin, rather gangly, and not particularly strong so he went down easily.

The sky was getting dark, and the first few stars were beginning to twinkle high above. The moon was already well above the horizon, bright and full and giving off enough light for me to be able to see pretty clearly.

I fought through several more vampires trying to make their way into the mansion. It felt as if we were making headway for a short while, at least until a second wave of vampires swooped in on the perimeter of the property.

They were carrying much bigger guns than the first wave had been.

I stiffened, knowing that things were about to get far more intense. They didn't wait to begin pulling the trigger. The constant pop of gunfire echoed heavy in the air, and it was quickly returned by my shifter family. The vampires screeched in agony once my garlic-soaked wooden bullets struck them at first and those screams only grew louder when they began to splinter inside them. Several of them paused long enough for the sentries above to shoot a sunfire bullet straight into their skulls, but they didn't get them all.

I dove into the fray, trying to take care of as many of them that I could. They were caught off guard by me and I took advantage of that, driving my stake into one Venuti Clan member after the next. Lawson followed after me, his snarls vicious as he tore into the monsters that threatened his pack. It seemed to be going well and I began to hope that all of us were going to see this through. I ignored the sweat dripping down my back and focused on knocking out a particularly nasty fighter that had taken down at least one or two of the wolves.

I met his eyes and he knelt down, cocking his head to the side like a slithering snake. I grimaced, studying his graceful movements as he slinked in my direction. He was tall and lanky, but the muscles of his arms were solid. His red eyes bore into mine, and a wicked smile spread across his lips that left me feeling chilled.

I didn't like it. He was going to have to die next.

I waited for him to come to me. Cocky monsters like him couldn't resist a fight. I slid my hands along my belt, remembering the knife in my vest. I didn't want to use that yet. There was one last clip of sunfire bullets, and I swiftly loaded it into one of my guns. The vamp had chosen that moment of distraction to race toward me, but I'd expected that and when he was within a few steps of me, I turned quickly on my feet so that he rushed past me in his haste. I leveled my sight with the back of his head and pulled the trigger, ending him in less time than it took for me to draw in a breath. My only regret was not being able to see the look on his arrogant face when he realized that I had won.

The battle raged on all around me. When it finally ended, there were going to be a great many dead, both wolf and vampire alike. The constant gunfire and ceaseless screaming would haunt me for a long time, but now was not the time to focus on that.

I had to kill as many of the Venuti as I could. They'd killed my father and now they were trying to kill my second family. I wasn't going to let them.

I used the rest of my bullets to take out several more vamps that were carrying heavy-looking guns. They exploded in a brilliant show of light, and I moved on quickly, knowing that every second counted in this battle between the Venuti and the Crescent Moon Pack.

Without warning, a group of vampires surrounded me. Out of bullets and armed only with a wooden stake, I quickly realized that I was outnumbered, and things were about to get rough. The vampires consisted of both men and women, all very strong and from the looks of it, quite old. Their skin had an opaque papery consistency, more so than most vampires. I also noticed that the red in their eyes wasn't quite as bright as the younger ones, almost a dull blood red rather than the brilliant scarlet of a freshly sired vamp.

One of them walked forward and looked me up and down. There was something familiar about her, but I couldn't quite put my finger on it.

She looked like she'd come from money, her black pantsuit some designer label that I didn't remember the name of. The fabric was covered in muted gray stripes, making her appear tall and lean, and accentuating the elegant curves of her body along with it. Her eyes weren't like the others, bright red and intense as she stared back at me. Long blonde hair wound down her back, soft waves that probably took a long time to perfect. She was really quite pretty, but I could sense nothing but danger as she peered back at me.

"I didn't expect to see the likes of you here in the wolf's den," she purred, and I didn't like how unsettled her voice made me. I swallowed bravely and lifted my chin, gazing back at her with a look just as hard as hers.

"Well. Surprise," I quipped brazenly, not caring that the rest of the vamps around me stiffened at the challenge in my voice.

Her eyes hardened and she cocked her head to the side, appraising me with interest. Her expression was cold and unfeeling. The other Venuti kept looking toward her and I quickly realized that she was the one in charge of this massive attack.

"Ethan Winters' daughter," she murmured, her voice laced with expectation. "Now you are most certainly a prize."

She lifted a finger and a vampire grabbed me from behind. I reacted solely on instinct and lurched forward, throwing the unfortunate soul straight over my shoulder. It turned out the one that had grabbed me had been a woman and when she landed flat on her back, I forcefully stabbed a stake right through her heart.

I stood back up, taking my bloody stake along with it.

I stared back at the woman, rolling my upper lip in her direction. I studied her face a bit more, taking note of the high curve of her cheekbones and the plumpness of her lips. When she was alive, she'd probably paid for her fair share of plastic surgery.

"My name is Ava Winters. Who are you?" I asked boldly.

Her smile widened.

"Lola Claiborne," she answered simply.

Immediately, I recognized her last name. Her father was the governor of Louisiana. He was well liked by the human faction, but his daughter's reputation had followed him around like a dark cloud. She liked to spend money and party in the quarter like it was going out of style. More than once, she'd walked out on a tab or left a hotel room a mess and her father had needed to deal with it for her with an endless amount of dollar bills.

Apparently, it had finally caught up to her and the Venuti had taken her for themselves, probably to get the governor on their side.

She began to circle me, and I followed suit.

I could tell from the swiftness in her movements that she was still a fairly young vampire. She still wasn't used to humanizing the way she moved, each one happening a bit too quickly and a bit disjointed to the eye. Her fledgling status would mean that she would be harder to kill and stronger than most of the others.

I wasn't about to back down though.

I could sense Lawson on the outside. His incessant growls of fury were met with shrieking from the vampires, but I knew he was working his way in. Toboe's snarls joined his, and before long there was a small group of shifters trying to break into the circle that held me captive.

I decided to focus solely on Lola. She'd moved slightly closer to me, and I focused on her steps, memorizing the speed and distance between each one. They were shortening as she grew closer, and I took a step outward in order to make her work a bit harder. She chuckled quietly and I quickly jumped in her direction to test her reaction time and speed.

She was prepared for me and swung outward, but as she did so, I noticed her fumble a bit on her left ankle.

I'd remember that.

"You should join us, Ava. We'd treat you like a queen in the ranks of the Venuti," she murmured.

"I'd rather die," I snarled, and her grin grew wickedly. A cold chill passed over me at the sight of her pointed teeth as she stared directly at the vein in my neck.

"I could arrange that first," she threatened, and I practically snarled at her myself.

"It was my idea to turn your father into a monster," she replied quietly, lifting her fingers and studying the red of her painted nails like they were the most interesting thing in the world.

"Your idea?" I scoffed.

"It was something my lover and I came up with together to force my father into an unbreakable alliance with the Venuti. It was the perfect way for me to become a vampire in the most spectacular way too," she replied.

"Your lover?"

"Nicolai. I think you might remember him. You're the one that shot one of your fancy bullets straight into his skull," she snarled.

I grimaced and her face turned dark.

"I'd planned to come for you and make you suffer for killing him, but I'm delighted to get that chance far sooner than I anticipated. I'm going to enjoy this," she murmured, lifting her chin. Her eyes glinted with a deranged delight, and I took a step back, trying to figure out my next move.

At that moment, Lawson and Toboe leapt forward and landed on top of the shoulders of a couple of small vamps in the ring. Without even a second's hesitation, they tore through them, and I took advantage of that momentary distraction to rush straight at Lola.

She tried to swerve away from me, but I'd expected that. I kicked her left ankle as hard as I could and when she attempted to twist away from me, she crumpled just enough for me to grab at her upper arm and throw her to the side.

All her life, she'd been primped and cared for. She hadn't trained like I had. Sure, she was a vampire, but she wasn't prepared to fight against the likes of me.

I wound my arm around her neck and practically dragged her up by it. She sputtered and coughed, but I didn't show her any mercy. With practiced swiftness, I pulled the sunfire knife from my belt and pressed it against her throat just hard enough to elicit a single droplet of blood.

She froze, suddenly realizing that she was in far deeper than she thought she was.

"You can't kill me with a knife," she spat viciously, but I detected just the slightest grain of fear in the way her voice shook.

"This isn't just a knife," I answered simply.

The wolves descended on the vampires surrounding me, ripping them apart and decimating their ranks in a coordinated attack. The Venuti had no time to recover and for a fraction of a second, Lawson held my gaze with his.

"End her. Make her pay for what she did to your father."

I didn't need to be told twice.

My hand flew back and with every single ounce of strength left in me, I buried the blade of that knife straight into Lola's skull. She screamed, but there wasn't enough time for her to stop what was coming. My thumb wound around the base and pressed the button at the bottom firmly and it clicked.

Just like the sunfire bullets, a massive ball of light started to consume her. It was far larger and so bright that it mimicked the rising of the sun in the dead of night. Her remains sizzled away in the savage heat and she collapsed to the ground as the light began to fade away. All that was left was a headless corpse in the end.

I stared down at her for a long time. Lola and Nicolai were the entire reason behind my father's death. Now that both of them were dead, I felt like I could breathe, like a massive weight had been taken from my shoulders and I sighed quietly in my victory.

I knew what had happened now. I knew my father wasn't a monster and that was all I wanted in the end.

The world went silent. The vampires stopped fighting. I'd killed their leader and they were standing around now, listless and uncertain.

I began to speak.

"I want the remaining Venuti to take a message back to their leaders," I began. Lawson and Toboe moved to either side of me, sitting down and observing all around me.

"You will leave the quarter and never come back. The Venuti have lost New Orleans and it is now the territory of the Crescent Moon Pack. Find refuge elsewhere. You are no longer welcome here."

I stayed silent for a moment, letting my words resonate all around me.

"Additionally, if a Venuti Clan member wanders into our city without special permission, they will have signed their own death warrant. There will be no feeding on locals, no more killing of tourists so that you can eat. None of that. You will leave and *never* come back," I shouted, and the vampires took a step back.

I looked around, taking in the expressions of all of them watching me. Some were terrified, others furious, and yet even more seemed to be ambivalent.

"Now go," I roared.

Slowly, the vampires began to disappear, one by one, several pairs and even a few small groups took off together. Before long, the only people left were the shifters and me.

In the minutes that followed, I stayed silent, watching as the wolves gathered in front of me in a massive group. I looked out at them, and they all lifted their heads, howling in unison for me.

It was more than just a simple howl. It was the manifestation of their respect for me as their alpha's mate, as their leader in my own way and my heart swelled with love and loyalty for every single one of them.

I was truly one of them now.

"You were wonderful, mate. I'm so proud of you," Lawson told me.

I smiled, feeling nothing but love in my heart. I reached for my alpha, climbing up onto his back. He made his way back toward the house, taking me away from battle and back into the safety of my new home.

CHAPTER 11

Lawson

The days following the battle were hectic and hollow. I had to bury more than fifty of my wolves and that settled heavy on me. I hated losing my own, but I knew I had to bear that weight and stay strong as the leader of my pack. Ava put together a touching ceremony honoring those who gave their lives to protect the pack. It was beautiful, but even in our overwhelming sorrow, Ava shone like a beacon among us. She remained her spirited self despite everything she'd gone through and that made me the happiest man alive.

I touched her, kissed her lips, and told her how much I loved her every chance I got. There would be time for us soon, but there was much to deal with in the aftermath of war.

The battle against the Venuti had garnered media attention, but with some swift work on Genzo's part, he was able to change the narrative to one of a gang war that had spiraled out of control. We disposed of all the vampire corpses through various avenues, my favorite being a shipping container on a storage vessel that was going to be accidentally sunk in the middle of the Gulf.

There was a significant amount of damage to my home and the surrounding landscape. I met with several local contractors and had them get to work as quickly as possible. Additionally, weapon stocks needed to be replenished just in case the Venuti were dumb enough to challenge us again. Fortunately, it appeared they'd run off with their tails in between their legs. There were no signs of their existence in the quarter, not in the bars, the shops, or even the ports along the Mississippi. My men patrolled the rest of the city, looking for any sign of them and finding none.

The city was ours.

However, I knew the Venuti. They'd been around for a very long time and even though we'd destroyed a fair number of them, there were many more waiting in the ranks. They'd retreated for now. I wasn't sure for how long or if they'd stay out of New Orleans forever. I'd enjoy this temporary reprieve however long it lasted, but I would be prepared if they chose to come at me once again.

Two weeks later, I picked up the phone and called the Council.

The Council had existed for centuries. It was an organization of all the families in the world, shifter and vampire alike. It was only a matter of time before they came calling and I wanted to be the one to reach out to them first. As the alpha of the Crescent Moon Pack, one of the most formidable shifter families in the world, it was within my power to call a meeting of all the reigning kingpins in the United States.

That meeting happened three days later.

I didn't go alone. I brought Ava along with me.

I dressed her in a very expensive Christian Dior dress. It was blood red, edged with decadent lace, and tight enough to show off every curve of her body. It was designed in a way that showcased my mark on her shoulder, ensuring that it was clearly presented so no one could question that she was my mate.

I took her arm with mine and walked into the massive southern home on the edges of the city. I was guided into a central dining room. The Council had prepared a full meal for the shifter families. For the vampires, there were several goblets full of fresh warm blood. I tried not to turn my nose up at the scent of it, but it was rather rank.

It only worsened when the other figureheads started taking their seats at the table. I chose to sit at the head of the table, moving a chair closer to me so that Ava could sit alongside me. The table slowly filled until at long last, a representative of the Venuti walked through the door.

I studied his face. I already knew his name.

Vincenzo Lozano was a particularly vicious vampire. When he was a human, he'd fought and died in the Civil War. The uneasy years that followed proved to work in his favor and I knew of at least a dozen small massacres that he'd been a central part of. His reputation preceded him, and I knew he would be even more difficult to deal with than Nicolai had been if things went sour between us.

I didn't plan on allowing that to happen. Today, I was going to expose the Venuti's master plan of an all-out war between the wolf shifter families and the vampire clans.

When everyone was seated, I looked around the room. The men and women here in this room with me had the power to destroy North America with a phone call or a snap of the fingers. We could crash the stock market, empty every single bank in the country, or bring world trade to a close. Our power wasn't restrained by the borders of the United States. It went much farther than that, extending into Europe, Asia, Australia, and the rest of the world.

A group of waitresses surrounded the table, pouring glasses of whiskey or wine for the wolves and passing goblets of blood to the vampires. When everyone was served, I cleared my throat and I peered around the room, meeting eyes with each powerhouse at that table.

Cole, the leader of the Gray Ridge Pack and also a close ally of mine, dragged his gaze from me to Ava with a knowing look. He finally grinned and I returned the sentiment. There were several more wolf families that acknowledged my mate silently, but I planned to introduce her publicly to all of them.

"I'd like to welcome all the families to this meeting of the Council. We have much to discuss, so if it's convenient for everyone here, I'd like to begin," I said boldly. The table quieted and all eyes fell on me. I didn't miss the vindictive glare in Vincenzo's red eyes either.

I'd have to watch out for him.

"The first order of business I'd like to bring to the table is the woman sitting beside me. She is my mate and as such, she is my responsibility."

"She should pay for what she did to Nicolai," Vincenzo spat.

I glared in his direction.

"I have dealt with her in the way that wolves deal with their mates. That matter has been settled to my satisfaction." With a sidelong glance, I saw Ava dip her head and I was pleased to see a pink blush spread across her pretty cheeks. She showed the room a demure sense of a punished and very contrite mate by my side.

"Not to mine," Vincenzo growled. I took Ava's hand in my own and stared back at Vincenzo, challenging him in silence with just a look.

"Since you spoke up so quickly, Vincenzo, why don't we discuss why she got involved with the Venuti Clan in the first place? Why don't you tell the Council what you were trying to contract her father to do for you?" I pressed.

With a furious glare, he went quiet.

"Why don't I tell them myself then, Vincenzo?" I said, sitting back with a hard look in his direction. He didn't speak up anymore and the other families appeared ready to listen.

I started to tell the story, explaining how the Venuti had tried to contract Ava's father to create weapons for them that would be detrimental to wolf shifters. I explained the silver-tipped bullets, the studies into the application of wolfsbane, as well as a number of other high-tech weapons they wanted.

I told them that her father had refused, and that the Venuti had forced him to do what he did that day. I didn't detail the massacre. I didn't want to in front of Ava, but the mention of her father's name was enough for the surrounding Council members to suck in a halted breath.

They knew who he was. They knew what he did.

I continued without pause.

"The evidence we found in the Venuti tower was damning. Not only were they coming after the Crescent Moon Pack, but they had intentions to go to war with every wolf family in the country. After that, they intended to expand throughout the world," I continued.

Everyone at that table turned toward Vincenzo.

"If you need to see what we found, my beta is here with me. He has a copy of the extensive records that the Venuti kept on this topic," I added.

"I don't think that is necessary. After the meeting is concluded, the evidence can be circulated amongst us so that everyone here can see it," Cole said. A chorus of agreement echoed around the table.

The leader of the Asamire Clan quietly looked from me to Vincenzo. I knew a little about their family, but not much and they liked it that way. From my understanding, they were a vampire clan of pretty badass assassins. They were generally quiet and liked to be surrounded in an air of mystery. They didn't cause trouble though. They kept to themselves. I didn't know his name, but the way he stared at Vincenzo revealed just how disgusted he was in the behavior of his fellow vampire.

Even the king of the Lasombre Clan sat back with an air of annoyance. He was dressed in all black, as vampires from his clan generally were. They had just as much power as the Venuti, but they usually fought amongst their own clan rather than with anyone else.

"We don't want war with the families. What can we do to avoid this?" the Asamire kingpin said, his voice quiet but powerful all the same.

Ava cleared her throat.

"My mate would like to speak on behalf of the Crescent Moon Pack," I offered, and she stood up beside me, pressing her fingers against the table.

"It is our demand that the Venuti fully surrender the city of New Orleans. They will conduct business in their own territory and never set foot in ours again."

"That's bullshit. She's nothing but a human," Vincenzo spat.

"She's my human," I growled. "She bears my mark on her neck and you will treat her the same as you would anyone sitting at this table."

Cole slammed his hand on the table.

"Enough, Vincenzo. The members of your clan are guilty of the intention of starting a war that would involve everyone sitting at this table. If you continue, all of us here will have to vote on the ending of the Venuti family name."

He hadn't said it, but the threat of extermination was ripe in the air. In the history of the world, only one family had ever been exterminated, the vampire clan responsible for the Dark Ages in the human world. No one spoke of their family name because it had been lost centuries ago, wiped from history and forever from memory.

"Both Nicolai and Lola Claiborne are dead. Much to our knowledge, they were the two vampires that were responsible for both Ava's father's death and the stoking of war between the families," I continued. "I wanted to ensure that the Council was aware of such dangerous behavior so that if anything more came of it, we all would be ready to deal with it."

"I agree," Cole echoed.

"I would also like to ask for a contract of peace between my pack and the Venuti. I want their detailed surrender and retreat from New Orleans documented, so that if anything further occurs in the future, a written record is kept," I added.

The men at the table nodded in agreement. Ava sat back down beside me.

Vincenzo continued to glare at me, but I no longer cared. I knew this meeting wouldn't resolve anything more than an uneasy peace agreement between us and that he could turn around and attack my pack tomorrow.

The rest of the families had needed to know what they were up to though so that they could make their own preparations too.

Under the table, Ava slid her fingers in mine and squeezed them tight. Beside me, she lifted her chin with pride.

I turned my head, admiring the way her pretty blue eyes sparkled beneath her long lashes. Her hair hung down her back in waves, soft and supple. She turned to me with a smirk edging at the corners of her lips. The tip of her tongue slid slowly along her upper lip, and she turned back to the table, watching the proceeding with a regal air that I hadn't seen radiate from her ever before.

Her shoulders were pulled back and her chin was held high. I glanced around the table once more and saw that the other family heads were looking back at her with respect and admiration, like she belonged there.

I grinned.

She did belong there.

I was king of the Crescent Moon Pack. She was my mate, but that's not all she was.

She was also my queen.

EPILOGUE

Ava

I felt like it had been weeks since Lawson had touched me. Time had flown after the vampire attack. There was so much to do. Many of the wolves had gotten wounded and I took it upon myself to help treat a great number of them. The meeting of the Council had gone much better than expected. The peace agreement had been drawn up and signed by all attending parties, fully recording the events the Venuti had put into motion.

With a sigh, I leaned over the balcony, taking in the fresh flowers that had been planted along the house and across the rolling hills in front of my home. I'd planted a number of my favorites, including several purple lilac bushes, sunflowers, and a number of gardenias along the walkways. It all came together so beautifully in the end that I found myself admiring it from time to time from the balcony off of our bedroom.

"When the light hits you just right, little mate, I can see right through that thin silky nightgown," Lawson said from behind me. I turned my head with a smirk.

His arms wrapped around my waist, gliding down to grip the hem. He lifted it slowly, baring me inch by inch until he had it gathered well above my hips.

"Lawson!" I shrieked, trying to grab my nightgown and lower it back down.

"Little mate, it's been some time since I reminded you of your rightful place, hasn't it?" he purred, and my legs felt weak.

"Yes, alpha," I whispered.

"Bend over and grip the railing. I'm going to turn this pretty little bottom bright pink, just because I want to. If you take your spanking like a very good girl, you just may earn my cock inside that greedy little pussy after I'm through. If you're a bad girl though, you're going to take me in that tight little bottom of yours," he growled and I shivered hotly, chewing my lip.

I had a decision to make.

I wanted to feel his hands all over me. Already, my clit was throbbing with anticipation of his touch. I swallowed uncertainly, glancing up toward him. His yellow eyes were almost golden, sparkling with his own desire.

Did I want to be a good girl, or did I want to be a bad girl?

His eyes glinted, and I knew at once what I wanted. I didn't need gentle. I needed my alpha. I needed my beast.

"Make me," I dared him.

"Oh, little mate, I'm going to enjoy this," he grinned, and I lifted my chin in defiance.

I didn't tell him, but I was going to enjoy this too.

The End

AFTERWORD

Stormy Night Publications would like to thank you for your interest in our books.

If you liked this book (or even if you didn't), we would really appreciate you leaving a review on the site where you purchased it. Reviews provide useful feedback for us and our authors, and this feedback (both positive comments and constructive criticism) allows us to work even harder to make sure we provide the content our customers want to read.

If you would like to check out more books from Stormy Night Publications, if you want to learn more about our company, or if you would like to join our mailing list, please visit our website at:

http://www.stormynightpublications.com

BOOKS OF THE ALPHA BROTHERHOOD SERIES

Savage

Many men have tried to master me, but never one like Aric. He is not just an alpha, he is a fearsome beast, and he means to take for himself what warriors and kings could not conquer.

I thought I could fight him, but his mere presence forced overwhelming, unimaginable need upon me and now it is too late. I'm about to go into heat, and what comes next will be truly shameful.

He's going to ravage me, ruthlessly laying claim to every single inch of me, and it's going to hurt. But no matter how desperately I plead as he wrenches one screaming climax after another from my helplessly willing body, he will not stop until I'm sore, spent, and marked as his.

It will be nothing short of savage.

Primal

I escaped the chains of a king. Now a far more fearsome brute has claimed me.

The Brotherhood gave him the right to breed me, but that is not why I am naked, wet, and sore.

My bottom bears the marks of his hard, punishing hand because I defied my alpha.

My body is slick with his seed and my own arousal because he took me anyway.

He didn't use me like a king enjoying a subject. He took me the way a beast claims his mate.

It was long, hard, and painfully intense, but it was much more than that.

It was primal.

Rough

I came here as a spy. I ended up as the king's property.

I was captured and locked in a dungeon, but it was only when I saw Magnar that I felt real fear.

He is a warrior and a king, but that is not why my virgin body quivers as I stand bare before him.

He is not merely an alpha. He is my alpha.

The one who will punish and master me.

The one who will claim and ravage me.

The one who will break me, but only after he's made me beg for it.

Wild

She's going to scream for me and I don't care who hears it.

I traveled to this city to disrupt the plans of the Brotherhood's enemies, not tame a defiant omega, but the moment Revna challenged me I knew punishing her would not be enough.

Despite her blushing protests, I'm going to bare her beautiful body and mark her quivering bottom with my belt, but she won't be truly put in her place until I put her flat on her back.

I'm her alpha and I will use her as I please.

BOOKS OF THE OMEGABORN TRILOGY

Frenzy

Inside the walls I was a respected scientist. Out here I'm vulnerable, desperate, and soon to be at the mercy of the beasts and barbarians who rule these harsh lands. But that is not the worst of it.

When the suppressants that keep my shameful secret wear off, overwhelming, unimaginable need will take hold of me completely. I'm about to go into heat, and I know what comes next…

But I'm not the only one with instincts far beyond my control. Savage men roam this wilderness, driven by their very nature to claim a female like me more fiercely than I can imagine, paying no heed to my screams as one brutal climax after another is ripped from my helplessly willing body.

It won't be long now, and when the mating starts, it will be nothing short of a frenzy.

Frantic

Naked, bound, and helplessly on display, my arousal drips down my bare thighs and pools at my feet as the entire city watches, waiting for the inevitable. I'm going into heat, and they know it.

When the feral beasts who live outside the walls find me, they will show my virgin body no mercy. With my need growing more desperate by the second, I'm not sure I'll want them to…

By the time the brutes arrive to claim and ravage me, I'm going to be absolutely frantic.

Fever

I've led the Omegaborn for years, but the moment these brutes arrived from beyond the wall I knew everything was about to change. These beasts aren't here to take orders from me, they're here to take me the way I was meant to be taken, no matter how desperately I resist what I need.

Naked, punished, and sore, all I can do is scream out one savage, shameful climax after another as my body is claimed, used, and mastered. I'm about to learn what it means to be an omega…

MAFIA AND BILLIONAIRE ROMANCES BY
SARA FIELDS

Fear

She wasn't supposed to be there tonight. I took her because I had no other choice, but as I carried her from her home dripping wet and wearing nothing but a towel, I knew I would be keeping her.

I'm going to make her tell me everything I need to know. Then I'm going to make her mine.

She'll sob as my belt lashes her bottom and she'll scream as climax after savage climax is forced from her naked, quivering body, but there will be no mercy no matter how shamefully she begs.

She's not just going to learn to obey me. She's going to learn to fear me.

On Her Knees

Blaire Conrad isn't just the most popular girl at Stonewall Academy. She's a queen who reigns over her subjects with an iron fist. But she's made me an enemy, and I don't play by her rules.

I make the rules, and I punish my enemies.

She'll scream and beg as I strip her, spank her, and force one brutal climax after another from her beautiful little body, but before I'm done with her she'll beg me shamefully for so much more.

It's time for the king to teach his queen her place.

Boss

The moment Brooke Mikaels walked into my office, I knew she was mine. She needed my help and thought she could use her sweet little body to get it, but she learned a hard lesson instead.

I don't make deals with silly little girls. I spank them.

She'll get what she needs, but first she'll moan and beg and scream with each brutal climax as she takes everything I give her. She belongs to me now, and soon she'll know what that means.

His Majesty

Maximo Giovanni Santaro is a king. A real king, like in the old days. The kind I didn't know still existed. The kind who commands obedience and punishes any hint of defiance from his subjects.

His Majesty doesn't take no for an answer, and refusing his royal command has earned me not just a spanking that will leave me sobbing, but a lesson so utterly shameful that it will serve as an example for anyone else who might dare to disobey him. I will beg and plead as one brutal, screaming climax after another ravages my quivering body, but there will be no mercy for me.

He's not going to stop until he's taught me that my rightful place is at his feet, blushing and sore.

Pet

Even before Chloe Banks threw a drink in my face in front of a room full of powerful men who know better than to cross me, her fate was sealed. I had already decided to make her my pet.

I would have taught her to obey in the privacy of my penthouse, but her little stunt changed that.

My pet learned her place in public instead, blushing as she was bared, sobbing as she was spanked, and screaming as she was brought to one brutal, humiliating climax after another.

But she has so many more lessons to learn. Lessons more shameful than she can imagine.

She will plead for mercy as she is broken, but before long she will purr like a kitten.

Blush for Daddy

"Please spank me, Daddy. Please make it hurt."

Only a ruthless bastard would make an innocent virgin say those words when she came to him desperate for help, then savor every quiver of her voice as she begs for something so shameful.

I didn't even hesitate.

I made Keri Esposito's problems go away. Then I made her call me daddy.

The image of that little bottom bare over my lap was more than I could resist, and the thought of her kneeling naked at my feet to thank me properly afterwards left me as hard as I've ever been.

Maybe I'm a monster, but I saw the wet spot on her panties before I pulled them down.

She didn't come to my door just for the kind of help only a powerful billionaire could offer.

She came because she needed me to make her blush for daddy.

Reckoning

Dean Waterhouse was supposed to be a job. Get in. Get married. Take his money and get out.

But he came after me.

Now I'm bound to his bed, about to learn what happens to naughty girls who play games.

The man who put his ring on my finger was gentle. The man who tracked me down is not.

He's going to make me blush, beg, and scream for him.

Then he's going to make me call him daddy.

BOOKS OF THE VAKARRAN CAPTIVES SERIES

Conquered

I've lived in hiding since the Vakarrans arrived, helping my band of human survivors evade the aliens who now rule our world with an iron fist. But my luck ran out.

Captured by four of their fiercest warriors, I know what comes next. They'll make an example of me, to show how even the most defiant human can be broken, trained, and mastered.

I promise myself that I'll prove them wrong, that I'll never yield, even when I'm stripped bare, publicly shamed, and used in the most humiliating way possible.

But my body betrays me.

My will to resist falters as these brutes share me between the four of them and I can't help but wonder if soon, they will conquer my heart…

Mastered

First the Vakarrans took my home. Then they took my sister. Now, they have taken me.

As a prisoner of four of their fiercest warriors, I know what fate awaits me. Humans who dare to fight back the way I did are not just punished, they are taught their place in ways so shameful I shudder to think about them.

The four huge, intimidating alien brutes who took me captive are going to claim me in every way possible, using me more thoroughly than I can imagine. I despise them, yet as they force one savage, shattering climax after another from my naked, quivering body, I cannot help but wonder if soon I will beg for them to master me completely.

Ravaged

Though the aliens were the ones I always feared, it was my own kind who hurt me. Men took me captive, and it was four Vakarran warriors who saved me. But they don't plan to set me free…

I belong to them now, and they intend to make me theirs more thoroughly than I can imagine.

They are the enemy, and first I try to fight, then I try to run. But as they punish me, claim me, and share me between them, it isn't long before I am begging them to ravage me completely.

Subdued

The resistance sent them, but that's not really why these four battle-hardened Vakarrans are here.

They came for me. To conquer me. To master me. To ravage me. To strip me bare, punish me for the slightest hint of defiance, and use my quivering virgin body in ways far beyond anything in even the very darkest of my dreams, until I've been utterly, completely, and shamefully subdued.

I vow never to beg for mercy, but I can't help wondering how long it will be until I beg for more.

Abducted

When I left Earth behind to become a Celestial Mate, I was promised a perfect match. But four Vakarrans decided they wanted me, and Vakarrans don't ask for what they want, they take it.

These fearsome, savagely sexy alien warriors don't care what some computer program thinks would be best for me. They've claimed me as their mate, and soon they will claim my body.

I planned to resist, but after I was stripped bare and shamefully punished, they teased me until at last I pleaded for the climax I'd been so cruelly denied. When I broke, I broke completely. Now they are going to do absolutely anything they please with me, and I'm going to beg for all of it.

BOOKS OF THE CAPTIVE BRIDES SERIES

Wedded to the Warriors

As an unauthorized third child, nineteen-year-old Aimee Harrington has spent her life avoiding discovery by government authorities, but her world comes crashing down around her after she is caught stealing a vehicle in an act of petulant rebellion. Within hours of her arrest, she is escorted onto a ship bound for a detention center in the far reaches of the solar system.

This facility is no ordinary prison, however. It is a training center for future brides, and once Aimee has been properly prepared, she will be intimately, shamefully examined and then sold to an alien male in need of a mate. Worse still, Aimee's defiant attitude quickly earns her the wrath of the strict warden, and to make an example of her, Aimee is offered as a wife not to a sophisticated gentleman but to three huge, fiercely dominant warriors of the planet Ollorin.

Though Ollorin males are considered savages on Earth, Aimee soon realizes that while her new mates will demand her obedience and will not hesitate to spank her soundly if her behavior warrants it, they will also cherish and protect her in a way she has never experienced before. But when the time comes for her men to master her completely, will she find herself begging for more as her beautiful body is claimed hard and thoroughly by all three of them at once?

Her Alien Doctors

After nineteen-year-old Jenny Monroe is caught stealing from the home of a powerful politician, she is sent to a special prison in deep space to be trained for her future role as an alien's bride.

Despite the public bare-bottom spanking she receives upon her arrival at the detention center, Jenny remains defiant, and before long she earns herself a trip to the notorious medical wing of the facility. Once there, Jenny quickly discovers that a sore bottom will now be the least of her worries, and soon enough she is naked, restrained, and shamefully on display as three stern, handsome alien doctors examine and correct her in the most humiliating ways imaginable.

The doctors are experts in the treatment of naughty young women, and as Jenny is brought ever closer to the edge of a shattering climax only to be denied again and again, she finds herself begging to be taken in any way they please. But will her captors be content to give Jenny up once her punishment is over, or will they decide to make her their own and master her completely?

Taming Their Pet

When the scheming of her father's political enemies makes it impossible to continue hiding the fact that she is an unauthorized third child, twenty-year-old Isabella Bedard is sent to a detainment facility in deep space where she will be prepared for her new life as an alien's bride.

Her situation is made far worse after some ill-advised mischief forces the strict warden to ensure that she is sold as quickly as possible, and before she knows it, Isabella is standing naked before two huge, roughly handsome alien men, helpless and utterly on display for their inspection. More disturbing still, the men make it clear that they are buying her not as a bride, but as a pet.

Zack and Noah have made a career of taming even the most headstrong of females, and they waste no time in teaching their new pet that her absolute obedience will be expected and even the slightest defiance will earn her a painful, embarrassing bare-bottom spanking, along with far more humiliating punishments if her behavior makes it necessary.

Over the coming weeks, Isabella is trained as a pony and as a kitten, and she learns what it means to fully surrender her body to the bold dominance of two men who will not hesitate to claim her in any way they please. But though she cannot deny her helpless arousal at being so thoroughly mastered, can she truly allow herself to fall in love with men who keep her as a pet?

Sold to the Beasts

As an unauthorized third child with parents who were more interested in their various criminal enterprises than they were in her, Michelle Carter is used to feeling unloved, but it still hurts when she is brought to another world as a bride for two men who turn out not to even want one.

After Roan and Dane lost the woman they loved, they swore there would never be anyone else, and when their closest friend purchases a beautiful human he hopes will become their wife, they reject the match. Though they are cursed to live as outcasts who shift into terrible beasts, they are not heartless, so they offer Michelle a place in their home alongside the other servants. She will have food, shelter, and all she needs, but discipline will be strict and their word will be law.

Michelle soon puts Roan and Dane to the test, and when she disobeys them her bottom is bared for a deeply humiliating public spanking. Despite her situation, the punishment leaves her shamefully aroused and longing for her new masters to make her theirs, and as the days pass they find that she has claimed a place in their hearts as well. But when the same enemy who took their first love threatens to tear Roan and Dane away from her, will Michele risk her life to intervene?

Mated to the Dragons

After she uncovers evidence of a treasonous conspiracy by the most powerful man on Earth, Jada Rivers ends up framed for a terrible crime, shipped off to a detention facility in deep space, and kept in solitary confinement until she can be sold as a bride. But the men who purchase her are no ordinary aliens. They are dragons, the kings of Draegira, and she will be their shared mate.

Bruddis and Draego are captivated by Jada, but before she can become their queen the beautiful, feisty little human will need to be publicly claimed, thoroughly trained, and put to the test in the most shameful manner imaginable. If she will not yield her body and her heart to them completely, the fire in their blood will burn out of control until it destroys the brotherly bond between them, putting their entire world at risk of a cataclysmic war.

Though Jada is shocked by the demands of her dragon kings, she is left helplessly aroused by their stern dominance. With her virgin body quivering with need, she cannot bring herself to resist as they take her hard and savagely in any way they please. But can she endure the trials before her and claim her place at their side, or will her stubborn defiance bring Draegira to ruin?

BOOKS OF THE TERRANOVUM BRIDES SERIES

A Gift for the King

For an ordinary twenty-two-year-old college student like Lana, the idea of being kidnapped from Earth by aliens would have sounded absurd... until the day it happened. As Lana quickly discovers, however, her abduction is not even the most alarming part of her situation. To her shock, she soon learns that she is to be stripped naked and sold as a slave to the highest bidder.

When she resists the intimate, deeply humiliating procedures necessary to prepare her for the auction, Lana merely earns herself a long, hard, bare-bottom spanking, but her passionate defiance catches the attention of her captor and results in a change in his plans. Instead of being sold, Lana will be given as a gift to Dante, the region's powerful king.

Dante makes it abundantly clear that he will expect absolute obedience and that any misbehavior will be dealt with sternly, yet in spite of everything Lana cannot help feeling safe and cared for in the handsome ruler's arms. Even when Dante's punishments leave her with flaming cheeks and a bottom sore from more than just a spanking, it only sets her desire for him burning hotter.

But though Dante's dominant lovemaking brings her pleasure beyond anything she ever imagined, Lana fears she may never be more than a plaything to him, and her fears soon lead to rebellion. When an escape attempt goes awry and she is captured by Dante's most dangerous enemy, she is left to wonder if her master cares for her enough to come to her rescue. Will the king risk everything to reclaim what is his, and if he does bring his human girl home safe and sound, can he find a way to teach Lana once and for all that she belongs to him completely?

A Gift for the Doctor

After allowing herself to be taken captive in order to save her friends, Morgana awakens to find herself naked, bound, and at the mercy of a handsome doctor named Kade. She cannot hide her helpless arousal as her captor takes his time thoroughly examining her bare body, but when she disobeys him she quickly discovers that defiance will earn her a sound spanking.

His stern chastisement and bold dominance awaken desires within her that she never knew existed, but Morgana is shocked when she learns the truth about Kade. As a powerful shifter and the alpha of his pack, he has been ordered by the evil lord who took Morgana prisoner to claim her and sire children with her in order to combine the strength of their two bloodlines.

Kade's true loyalties lie with the rebels seeking to overthrow the tyrant, however, and he has his own reasons for desiring Morgana as his mate. Though submitting to a dominant alpha does not come easily to a woman who was once her kingdom's most powerful sorceress, Kade's masterful lovemaking is unlike anything she has experienced before, and soon enough she is aching for his touch. But with civil war on the verge of engulfing the capital, will Morgana be torn from the arms of the man she loves or will she stand and fight at his side no matter the cost?

A Gift for the Commander

After she is rescued from a cruel tyrant and brought to the planet Terranovum, Olivia soon discovers that she is to be auctioned to the highest bidder. But before she can be sold, she must be trained, and the man who will train her is none other than the commander of the king's army.

Wes has tamed many human females, and when Olivia resists his efforts to bathe her in preparation for her initial inspection, he strips the beautiful, feisty girl bare and spanks her soundly. His stern chastisement leaves Olivia tearful and repentant yet undeniably aroused, and after the punishment she cannot resist begging for her new master's touch.

Once she has been examined Olivia's training begins in earnest, and Wes takes her to his bed to teach her what it means to belong to a dominant man. But try as he might, he cannot bring himself to see Olivia as just another slave. She touches his heart in a way he thought nothing could, and with each passing day he grows more certain that he must claim her as his own. But with war breaking out across Terranovum, can Wes protect both his world and his woman?

SCI-FI AND PARANORMAL ROMANCES BY SARA FIELDS

Feral

He told me to stay away from him, that if I got too close he would not be able to stop himself. He would pin me down and take me so fiercely my throat would be sore from screaming before he finished wringing one savage, desperate climax after another from my helpless, quivering body.

Part of me was terrified, but another part needed to know if he would truly throw me to the ground, mount me, and rut me like a wild animal, longer and harder than any human ever could.

Now, as the feral beast flips me over to claim me even more shamefully when I've already been used more thoroughly than I imagined possible, I wonder if I should have listened to him…

Inferno

I thought I knew how to handle a man like him, but there are no men like him. Though he is a billionaire, when he desired me he did not try to buy me, and when he wanted me bared and bound he didn't call his bodyguards. He did it himself, even as I fought him, because he could.

He told me soon I would beg him to ravage me… and I did. But it wasn't the pain of his belt searing my naked backside that drove me to plead with him to use me so shamefully I might never stop blushing. I begged because my body knew its master, and it didn't give me a choice.

But my body is not all he plans to claim. He wants my mind and my soul too, and he will have them. He's going to take so much of me there will be nothing left. He's going to consume me.

Manhandled

Two hours ago, my ship reached the docks at Dryac.

An hour ago, a slaver tried to drag me into an alley.

Fifty-nine minutes ago, a beast of a man knocked him out cold.

Fifty-eight minutes ago, I told my rescuer to screw off, I could take care of myself.

Fifty-five minutes ago, I felt a thick leather belt on my bare backside for the first time.

Forty-five minutes ago, I started begging.

Thirty minutes ago, he bent me over a crate and claimed me in the most shameful way possible.

Twenty-nine minutes ago, I started screaming.

Twenty-five minutes ago, I climaxed with a crowd watching and my bottom sore inside and out.

Twenty-four minutes ago, I realized he was nowhere near done with me.

One minute ago, he finally decided I'd learned my lesson, for the moment at least.

As he leads me away, naked, well-punished, and very thoroughly used, he tells me I work for him now, I'll have to earn the privilege of clothing, and I'm his to enjoy as often as he pleases.

Marked

I know how to handle men who won't take no for an answer, but Silas isn't a man. He's a beast who takes what he wants, as long and hard and savagely as he pleases, and tonight he wants me.

He's not even pretending he's going to be gentle. He's going to ravage me, and it's going to hurt.

I'll be spanked into quivering submission and used thoroughly and shamefully, but even when the endless series of helpless, screaming climaxes is finally over, I won't just be sore and spent.

I will be marked.

My body will no longer be mine. It will be his to use, his to enjoy, and his to breed, and no matter how desperate my need might grow in his absence, it will respond to his touch alone.

Forever.

Prize

Exiled from Earth by a tyrannical government, I was meant to be sold for use on a distant world. But Vane doesn't buy things. When he wants something, he takes it, and I was no different.

This alien brute didn't just strip me, punish me, and claim me with his whole crew watching. He broke me, making me beg for mercy and then for far more shameful things. Perhaps he would've been gentle if I hadn't defied him in front of his men, but I doubt it. He's not the gentle type.

When he carried me aboard his ship naked, blushing, and sore, I thought I would be no more than a trophy to be shown off or a plaything to amuse him until he tired of me, but I was wrong.

He took me as a prize, but he's keeping me as his mate.

Alpha

I used to believe beasts like him were nothing but legends and folklore. Then he came for me.

He is no mere alpha wolf. He is the fearsome expression of the virility of the Earth itself, come into the world for the first time in centuries to claim a human female fated to be his mate.

That human female is me.

When I ran, he caught me. When I fought him, he punished me.

I begged for mercy, but mercy isn't what he has in mind for me.

He's going to force one brutal climax after another from my naked, quivering body until my throat is sore from screaming and he's not going to stop until he is certain I know I am his.

Then he's going to breed me.

Thirst

Cain came for me today. Even before he spoke his name his power all but drove me to my knees.

Power that can pin me against a wall with just a thought and hold me there as he slowly cuts my clothes from my quivering body, making sure I know he is enjoying every blushing moment.

Power that will punish me until I plead for mercy, tease and torment me until I beg for release, and then ravage me brutally over and over again until I'm utterly spent and shamefully broken.

Power that will claim me as his forever.

MORE STORMY NIGHT BOOKS BY SARA FIELDS

Claimed by the General

When Ayala intervenes to protect a fellow slave-girl from a cruel man's unwanted attentions, she catches the eye of the powerful general Lord Eiotan. Impressed with both her boldness and her beauty, the handsome warrior takes Ayala into his home and makes her his personal servant.

Though Eiotan promises that Ayala will be treated well, he makes it clear that he expects his orders to be followed and he warns her that any disobedience will be sternly punished. Lord Eiotan is a man of his word, and when Ayala misbehaves she quickly finds herself over his knee for a long, hard spanking on her bare bottom. Being punished in such a humiliating manner leaves her blushing, but it is her body's response to his chastisement which truly shames her.

Ayala does her best to ignore the intense desire his firm-handed dominance kindles within her, but when her new master takes her in his arms she cannot help longing for him to claim her, and when he makes her his own at last, his masterful lovemaking introduces her to heights of pleasure she never thought possible.

But as news of the arrival of an invader from across the sea reaches the city and a ruthless conqueror sets his eyes on Ayala, her entire world is thrown into turmoil. Will she be torn from Lord Eiotan's loving arms, or will the general do whatever it takes to keep her as his own?

Kept for Christmas

After Raina LeBlanc shows up for a meeting unprepared because she was watching naughty videos late at night instead of working, she finds herself in trouble with Dr. Eliot Knight, her stern, handsome boss. He makes it clear that she is in need of strict discipline, and soon she is lying over his knee for a painful, embarrassing bare-bottom spanking.

Though her helpless display of arousal during the punishment fills Raina with shame, she is both excited and comforted when Eliot takes her in his arms after it is over, and when he invites her to spend the upcoming Christmas holiday with him she happily agrees. But is she prepared to offer him the complete submission he demands?

The Warrior's Little Princess

Irena cannot remember who she is, where she came from, or how she ended up alone in a dark forest wearing only a nightgown, but none of that matters as much as the fact that the vile creatures holding her captive seem intent on having her for dinner. Fate intervenes, however, when a mysterious, handsome warrior arrives in the nick of time to save her.

Darrius has always known that one day he would be forced by the power within him to claim a woman, and after he rescues the beautiful, innocent Irena he decides to make her his own. But the feisty girl will require more than just the protection Darrius can offer. She will need both his gentle, loving care and his firm hand applied to her bare bottom whenever she is naughty.

Irena soon finds herself quivering with desire as Darrius masters her virgin body completely, and she delights in her new life as his little girl. But Darrius is much more than an ordinary sellsword, and being his wife will mean belonging to him utterly, to be taken hard and often in even the most shameful of ways. When the truth of her own identity is revealed at last, will she still choose to remain by his side?

ABOUT THE AUTHOR

Do you want to read a FREE book?

Sign up for Sara Fields' newsletter and get a FREE copy of Sold to the Enemy!

https://www.sarafieldsromance.com/newsletter

About Sara Fields

Sara Fields is a USA Today bestselling romance author with a proclivity for dirty things, especially those centered in DARK, FANTASY, and ROMANCE. If you like science fiction, fantasy, reverse harem, menage, pet play and other kinky filthy things, all complete with happily-ever-afters, then you will enjoy her books.

Amazon
Bookbub
Facebook Page
Facebook Group
Email: otkdesire@gmail.com

Lightning Source UK Ltd.
Milton Keynes UK
UKHW010950040522
402470UK00004B/1019

9 798536 307502